Dark Desires

Measha Stone

Orzel Publishing

Dark Desires
Copyright © 2014 Measha Stone
Editor: Andrea Grimm
Cover Artist: SelfPubBookCovers.com/Warren

ISBN: 0-9905816-1-6
ISBN-13: 978-0-9905816-1-1

Dedication

To Billy, TJ and Tom.

CONTENTS

Acknowledgments

I deeply appreciate my family's unwavering support. Many nights of chicken nuggets and macaroni and cheese were eaten to make this book a reality. Thank you also, Tom at Three Spelling Mistakes for taking the time to read and give your honest thoughts on these stories in their earliest form. Your input was invaluable.

Dinner at Home

The phone rang repeatedly. The harsh sound echoed in the silent house. The machine picked up the call, the opening greeting played, and the beep prompted the caller to begin his message.

"I will assume you are home and are standing in the corner as I instructed. I will, also, assume that you have finished preparing dinner. I will be home in five minutes." The voice on the recording sounded harsh but held a tender quality that would be missed by most people.

The woman standing in the corner of the darkened dining room leaned her head against the wall. His voice embraced her. A shiver cascaded down her spine from a subtle draft leaking in from the closed window. She made a mental note to bring it up to him later.

Every order he left had been obeyed as he would see for himself when he arrived home in moments. She released a heavy sigh into the air. The wait seemed endless.

That morning, before he left for work, he'd given her his instructions for her day: two loads of laundry, clean the kitchen floor, check her emails, and have dinner prepared when he got home. She helped tie his tie and slipped his belt into the loops around his narrow waist. She smoothed the lapels of his suit jacket across his broad chest; she enjoyed feeling his hard muscles beneath her hands. The strength of him excited her.

They'd walked to the front door together where she kissed him goodbye, handed him his coffee, and watched from the doorway with a happy heart as he pulled out of the driveway. Their mornings had not always been so quiet and pleasing.

When they first married, there'd been strife and struggling for the reins of power. The love they shared while dating remained strong and pure, but their wills to conquer each other clashed. She became angered when he didn't listen to her but would become annoyed with him when he gave in to her demands.

The time came when he arrived at a decision. One of them would need to lead, and the other would need to follow. She found his new alpha attitude attractive. The conversation about rules and consequences made her panties wet. His promise to be strict and unwavering in his discipline gave her a rush she couldn't claim to have felt before. Along with his promise to be firm, came the assurance that he would reward her and treat her with all the respect she was due. Never would she feel second to him or any other in his life. From that moment, their marriage strengthened. Sex became hotter. Doing the dishes became a turn on. Laundry even set her into a dampness that wouldn't go away until he arrived home to help her relieve the pressure.

Once she locked the front door, having seen him off for the day, she went about performing her tasks for the day in her usual manner. She began with laundry and moved on to the cleaning the floors.

There was no real need for him to give her a task list for the day. At the age of thirty, she knew well enough how to take care of the house without his input, but it was part of what made their marriage work. The morning routine of his task list, and her kneeling before him to hear it, was only one of many rituals they performed together that kept their relationship strong and exciting. Doing the things he asked of her gave her a sense that he stood beside her as she worked. Feeling his presence throughout the day made it more meaningful, more pleasurable, than simply folding towels and washing dishes. She needed that, and he gave it to her with a willingness unmatched by any other.

She folded the last of the laundry after lunch and sat down at the computer to check her email. She found a message from him in her inbox. She smiled with excitement and clicked on the envelope to open his letter. He rarely emailed her during the day, unless he wanted to have fun with her that evening.

My Dearest,

We have been going along so nicely these past weeks. You have made me very proud; your behavior has been so good. I haven't had to punish you in a long time. I find that I am in need of some entertainment, however, and have chosen tonight, and you, for such an affair. Please keep in mind that you are NOT being punished in any way. I want you to understand this because I plan on spanking you a lot tonight, and I do not want you feel that you have disappointed me in any way.

That said, here are your instructions. Plan dinner as you would, but I want it ready and on the table when I walk in the door. Strip down completely. I don't want one inch of you clothed, and stand in the corner of the dining room. When I arrive home, do not look at me or speak. Tonight you are merely for my pleasure-my toy if you will.

She'd read the email several times before sitting back in her chair with a grin full of anticipation. This turn of events explained the devilish spark in his eyes at breakfast. She made quick order of wrapping up her chores and getting dinner started.

Now she stood naked in the corner of their dining

room when she heard the key slip into the front lock. She heard metal scraping against metal as the bolt of the door slid back in place; a chill ran down her spine at the soft jiggle of the door handle as he turned it. She felt her stomach knot when the door opened and his footsteps echoed in the front hallway. She bit her lower lip and took a deep calming breath to relax herself, unaware of what was to come put her nerves on edge.

Still in the front hall, he dropped his briefcase near the steps and hung his coat on the rack. He rifled through the mail lying on the small table near the entrance way, as though his wife were not standing naked in the dining room waiting to please him in any way he chose. She wanted to scream from the anticipation. He was purposely taking his time, and she wanted to growl her frustration.

When he entered the dining room, she imagined him puffing his chest out with pride at the sight of her. The soft light from the kitchen glistened on her skin. Even with the dim lighting in the dining room, she was sure he could make out every inch of her.

He walked around the table, running his hand over each chair as he passed; the clinking of his ring against the wood echoed in the room. He paused just behind her. She felt his eyes as they leisurely admired the beauty of her bottom.

She fidgeted from the heat his stare triggered in her. She wanted to turn her head to see him, to know that he was pleased, but she fought the urge. She reminded herself to breathe and nearly jumped when she felt his touch on her skin. He ran the tips of his fingers down her spine and cupped her bottom with his hands.

"You did as I instructed," he whispered in her ear.

She smiled and nodded.

He leaned further into her, and she could feel his hot breath on her neck. Anticipating his kiss, she tilted her head modestly.

He laughed and stepped back.

She sighed.

"Dinner smells wonderful," he complimented.

She remained silent as he took her hand in his and held it for moment before gently pulling her to face him.

"You read my email?" he asked, needlessly, as he held her chin in his hand.

She nodded, their gazes interlocked. When he was pleased with her, there was such warmth and love showing in his gaze she could easily lose herself there.

"Then you understand that I love you, and that we are having fun tonight?" he questioned. It seemed very important to him that she completely comprehend they were going to be enjoying themselves.

Although they took their marriage vows two years ago, it was only months before that they'd taken their roles of husband and wife in a different turn. She was still learning that pain and pleasure could exist simultaneously and that she would derive much gratification from such sessions.

She nodded again and ran her tongue over her lower lip. She wanted to throw her arms around him and kiss him, to smell him and to love him. Her expression always gave away what she wanted, and he smiled at her—the evilness of his intentions showing.

"You want me to kiss you," he stated as he ran his thumb over her lips with a silken touch.

She parted them slightly and nodded while trying to rub her cheek into his palm.

"Not yet, I think." He winked at her and dropped his hand from her face. Her shoulders sagged when he took his touch away. "Bend over the table," he instructed and turned her to face the long wooden table.

Obediently, she bent over the table. The freshly polished wood was cool against her breasts as she pressed down against the table. She rested her head, facing her right. Her hands lay flat on either side of her face. The coolness soothed her hot, blushing cheeks.

He ran his fingers over her bottom, and with a feather like touch traced her lower back. She felt his eyes on her again; he told her often that she was most beautiful when she was obedient. She hadn't spoken. She hadn't begged when he denied her what she wanted. She simply obeyed. She presented her bottom to him with the grace of royalty, knowing what was to come next and anticipating it.

He brought his hand back and was quick to deliver a volley of swats to her white skin. He didn't speak to her, didn't acknowledge the moans she was producing. He simply continued to reign down the slaps to her bottom. She imagined how her creamy white flesh blushed beneath the strokes.

His steady hand delivered lashes until he seemed satisfied the color and the warmth would not soon diminish. He helped her up with care and grasped her hands between his.

"Back to the corner with you." His soft eyes watched her obediently step back into her place. "Don't rub or I'll have to start over." His tone held warning and promise. "Hands on your head," he directed.

She managed a glimpse of his erection showing through his pants as she made her way to the corner. She wondered if he'd make it through the meal.

The lesson he'd been teaching her over the past several months was patience. She had none. Each time she gained a bit more, he rewarded her, and each time she pushed him, he punished her. She stood in the corner, aware that the evening ahead held the intentions of fun and play, but she knew the underlying lesson of patience joined in the games as well.

He took his seat at the burgundy table and neatly

placed his napkin on his lap before picking up the silverware. She'd prepared pot roast with roasted vegetables and mashed potatoes—his favorite of her meals. The clanking of the silverware against the plate paused between his bites; she squirmed with the knowledge that he was watching her.

"Did you eat?" He bit into a carrot.

"No, Sir," she answered into the corner. She could feel his eyes on her, staring at her well spanked bottom. She wiggled a bit for his amusement.

"Come here," he ordered with a soft tone.

She kept her hands planted on her head, and she walked to him with a seductive sway of her hips.

"Sit." He pointed to the floor beside him. She slid down to her knees and sat back on her heels. He looked down at her in silence for a long moment.

Her chestnut hair laid softly on her shoulders. Her supple breasts where raised from her hand position. The chill in the room perked her nipples to his attention. His warm eyes watched her as he plucked up a carrot with his fork and brought it to her lips.

"Open," he commanded and she obeyed.

She wrapped her lips around the carrot and pulled it from the fork with her teeth. She kept her eyes locked on his as she took her time chewing. She'd learned quickly that even a simple act such as eating a carrot could be done so in an alluring fashion. When she finished the carrot, she licked her lips. She wanted to grin when she saw the lust in his eyes, but she kept her expression somber. Her intense gaze fixed on him.

He patted her head and turned back to his meal. Every other bite he would feed her a small piece of vegetable or some of the meat. When he had eaten his fill, he pushed the plate away and began to sip on his drink. She had poured him a glass of his favorite wine when she carefully set the table before his arrival.

He reached down beside his chair to give her nipple a gentle squeeze and was quickly rewarded with a slight yelp from her lips. He set his glass on the table and gave her his full attention. He dragged his fingers along her jaw, traced her earlobe with his fingertips, and ran his thumb across her lips. She parted them slightly and began to lick at his thumb as he touched her.

She could feel his skin on her lips, and the craving she felt deep in her belly intensified. She wanted his touch on all of her; she needed him. He withdrew his thumb and turned his attention to her breasts. She filled his hands when he cupped them; he flicked her nipples with his thumbs.

She moaned slightly and arched her back a bit to give him more of her. She wanted everything he would give her, but she was not in control of their speed. He would decide when and where to touch her.

"I love your tits," he commented, and before she could respond, he gave each breast a sharp slap.

She shrank away from him.

"Do not move," he directed her in a firm tone.

His eyes were dark; she had not seen him so aroused before. She arched her back and closed her own eyes, unsure of what he was going to do next.

He flicked her nipples again, and without warning, he took her nipple between his fingers and began to pinch her.

She sucked in her breath and bit back the scream that raged in her throat. Just as she reached her limit, he released her. A burning sensation quickly replaced the sharpness of his fingers as the blood returned. She lost herself in the wave of emotions.

Opening her eyes, she sought out his gaze. Her mind reeled from the sensations while looking deeply into his stare. Each painful act would be lessened by his kiss, his touch, his eyes. He seemed to enjoy the switch

between pain and pleasure and was bent on teaching her
to enjoy it as well.

"Stand." He helped her to her feet. Once she was
settled in her position, he pushed away from the table to
face her. He ran his hand along her arm, down her belly,
and stopped when he reached the small patch of hair that
she kept so neatly trimmed for him.

"Open." He pinched her thighs. She quickly spread
her legs, and he gently ran his finger through the patch
of hair and downward until he was just above her
swollen arousal. He brushed her clit with his finger.

She gasped from the searing passion it brought to
her. Her cunt clenched at the idea of his touch. She
angled her hips to reach for him. He withdrew his hand.

"Oh." She pouted.

"We've only just begun." He turned her again to
face the table. He applied gentle pressure to her
shoulders until she was once again bent over the table.
He sat back in his chair and ran his hand over her
bottom. The heat from the first spanking no longer
lingered on her backside. He remedied that by giving her
several swats of his hand.

Then he reached between her legs and fondled her
slick, swollen clit. Her cunt pulsated with need; she
pushed her ass toward him. He removed his hand from
her and gave her a sharp slap to her backside. "On the
table."

She looked over her shoulder at him with
confusion.

"Go on. Up on the table. I want you to lay down."
He jabbed the surface with his fingers.

She gracefully lifted one knee and pushed herself
onto the top, turning over onto her back. She hoped she
looked more delicate than the act seemed.

The table felt cool beneath her freshly warmed
bottom, and she fidgeted until she found a comfortable

position. Her legs stuck straight out and her arms rested on either side of her. The chandelier hanging above her became her focal point. She hated the waiting.

She heard him moving about but didn't dare look at him. She heard his chair scrape against the hardwood floor and felt his warm hands on her ankles.

"I'm in the mood for some dessert." He smiled coyly as he pulled on her ankles, dragging her toward him. Her feet dangled off the table on either side of him; her backside sat on the very edge.

She looked down the length of her body and found him sitting in his chair with a piece of the chocolate cake she had baked.

"You will act as my plate." He plucked up the dessert and gently laid it on her nest of hair.

She groaned when a large crumb rolled down her lips and onto the table.

"I seem to have forgotten my fork." He laughed. "Well...I guess I'll just have to improvise."

She closed her eyes at the thought of what was about to happen. He'd mentioned to her in the past that he would use her as furniture or a plaything; it had seemed hot when he'd mentioned it. It didn't compare to the actual act. She felt outside herself. Heat rushed into her cheeks at the mental image of what was taking place in their dining room. She felt used, toyed with. It was exhilarating.

He took his time picking at the cake with his fingers, seeming to delight in the torment he caused. It was no coincidence he brushed against her clit often. She imagined his cock becoming harder with each moan she released into the room.

She did her best to keep still while he enjoyed his dessert. When there was not much of the cake left, he used his mouth to enjoy the chocolate. She sucked in her breath and almost bolted upright when she felt his tongue on her hot skin.

He was skilled in his movements as he twirled her clit in his mouth. He suckled the chocolate frosting off of her lips and licked her until the dessert was but a memory.

"Mmmm. That was delicious." He smiled over her mound at her. "Did you enjoy that, my pet?" He ran his hands up her thighs.

"Yes." She breathed out and tried to lift her hips up toward him, a near impossible feat with her feet dangling in the air.

He continued to run his hands over her thighs and tease her with his fingertips. He reached higher and cupped her breasts in his hands. Then he stood and bent over her elongated body to take a nipple into his mouth.

Again, she fought against a scream from the pleasure of it. He bit at her and suckled, while he playfully slapped the opposite breast.

"Roll onto your belly." He stood upright, leaving the cool air to assault her wet nipples.

She didn't want to. She knew what was coming next, and she would rather he continue to play with her tits. However, her wants were not the focus of the evening, so she followed his instructions.

She laid with her head resting on her folded hands and heard the clank of his buckle and the familiar sound of his belt being pulled from his pants. That sound usually sent horrible shivers down her spine when she had been naughty and was in trouble. He had never used his belt during play sessions. She worried she would not be able to stay still for him.

He gave no warning before the sting of the belt cascaded through her. She yelled out when it struck her for the second time across her thighs.

"Open your legs." His voice was impatient, and she slid her legs apart. He continued the whipping, methodically striking at her buttocks and her thighs.

She wiggled after each stroke and bucked a few times from the sting of it. She'd never taken so many strikes in a row before.

She focused on feeling each slash of the belt as he'd taught her. The electric heat shot up her back into her brain; she took a deep breath and waited for the next blow. The anxiousness that built from the waiting exploded into pieces when the leather lashed across her sore bottom. It was a round robin of excitement, anticipation, and pain over and again.

When he stopped and held the belt near her face, she felt the heat radiating from her bottom. "Hold this," he directed her, but when she reached her hand out for it, he retracted it.

"No, with your mouth," he clarified, and she opened her mouth for him. He placed the leather strap between her teeth, and she bit down on it, feeling the tears pooling in her eyes. He leaned down to kiss her, wiping her cheek with his forefinger. She felt his pride in his touch.

He whispered a few words of love and encouragement before he stood again and looked down at her. He tenderly ran his hands over her tingling bottom. "Such a good girl. You took those well. Your ass looks even sexier with my marks on your cheeks." He kissed a particularly tender spot. "So beautiful, " he whispered against her hot skin.

She groaned and lifted her hips, so her bottom rose off of the table. He laughed at her reaction, but she knew he was pleased with her willingness to give him her everything. He toyed with the warmth of her, the hot wetness that was there for the taking, before he drove his finger into her hard. She gasped and raised her bottom higher still.

He roughly moved his finger in and out of her. "My

little horny wife," he cooed. "That's it, move your hips just like that. Show me you love what I'm doing to you… Ah, I love that sound you make."

She raised her ass high in the air as she fucked his finger.

He smiled at her as she looked up at him with his belt still firmly planted between her teeth. Just as quickly as he'd invaded her body with his finger, he removed it from her. She blessed him with another groan of dissatisfaction.

"You are here for *my* enjoyment." He slapped her bottom harshly.

She whimpered.

"Turn over," he demanded, and before she had a chance to obey, he used his own hands to lift her hips and flip her onto her back as though she were a flapjack.

She saw something in his eyes shift. It wasn't anger, nor was he disappointed, but it was something else. She could not see his thoughts, and it worried her. She was giving her entire body over to him. She trusted him to do as he wished for his enjoyment, and that would ultimately gratify her own as well.

"Do you think you should have your legs open or closed?" he asked firmly.

She didn't respond, but merely opened her legs as wide as she could for him.

"I asked you a question." He slapped her breast when she remained silent.

She tried to speak, but the belt muffled her sounds. He took the belt and laid it across her breasts.

"Open, Sir," she stated meekly.

"And why is that?" he asked with a raised eyebrow.

"Closing my legs is the same as hiding my pussy from you," she answered while doing her best to keep her eyes locked with his. To say such a thing out loud filled her with embarrassment, and she had to force herself not to look away from him.

"That's right, and are you allowed to hide any part of your body from me?" he asked as he lifted the belt and folded it in half and then in half again.

"No, Sir." She shook her head, her gaze now directed at his hands playing with the leather.

"And why is that?" he asked as he lightly ran the end of the looped belt across her belly and down to her pussy.

"Because you own my body. Everything I have and am belongs to you," she whispered and closed her eyes when she saw him lift the belt again.

"Very good," he praised and brought the belt crashing down onto her clit.

She fought the urge to close her legs as he repeatedly brought the belt down again and again onto her exposed sex.

He gave her pussy five strokes of the belt before he told her once again to open her mouth and hold the weapon for him.

He strolled around the table until he stood between her legs. In one swift motion he pulled her until her bottom was once again on the edge of the table. She heard his zipper then his command. "Open your eyes." His voice thick with lust. She quickly obeyed. Her stare immediately focused on his dick that had been pulled free from his pants. "Look at me." His smile softened his demand. Their eyes locked as he drove into her hard.

She gripped the edges of the table as his thrusts found a rhythm. She moaned as he fucked her harder.

He lifted her legs, so he held her feet in the air. She thrashed her head from side to side with each thrust of his dick and felt the intensity build in her belly. She bucked under him as best she could and bit harder into the leather as she drew closer to her own climax.

"Do you want to come?" His voice was hoarse.

She nodded vigorously, and he laughed.

"Beg. But don't you dare drop my belt," he ordered through his ragged breathing.

She knew he could not make out most of what she said. His smile widened as did his pupils at the sounds she made for him.

"Come now!" he decreed, and she bucked harder up at him, her breasts bouncing harshly.

She bit into the leather as she screamed out in climax.

Once the orgasmic waves diminished, he pulled from her and laid his hand on her stomach. After giving her a moment to recover her senses, he smiled down at her. He pried the belt from her lips and helped her off of the table. A single finger pointed to the floor, and she obediently knelt before him.

"Open your mouth," he instructed. "I want you to wrap those pretty lips around my cock and suck it." He growled when he felt her hot tongue on his dick.

She hummed lightly as she sucked on him, taking him fully into her mouth, so the head of his cock could touch the back of her throat. She wrapped her right hand around his shaft and massaged him. She again took him deep into her mouth and retracted.

He stood in their dining room, his wife completely nude kneeling obediently before him, sucking on his dick because he had ordered her to. Because, she wanted nothing more at that moment than to please him.

He placed his hands on her head and entwined his fingers in her hair. His hips moved along with her rhythm. She made slurping noises, one of his favorite sounds. Her tongue slid over him and down his shaft; she intensified her grip on his dick as she continued to pleasure him. She felt his balls tighten.

His head touched the back of her throat once more before he let out a yell as he burst into her mouth, the warm liquid splashing onto her tongue and sliding down her throat.

She stopped in her movements and let him continue his rocking motions. He held tightly onto her as he climaxed. When he was finished, he sighed and released her hair to pull back from her. She licked her lips and went about using her tongue to clean him completely.

"God! I love you," he proclaimed with a gentle touch to her cheek.

She smiled at him with pride and sat back on her heels.

He helped her stand and kissed her deeply. "I am the luckiest man in the world," he whispered into her ear.

"And I am the luckiest of women," she whispered back, wrapping her arms around his waist.

"Upstairs with you," he ordered with a light slap to her bottom.

She looked at him with a little bit of confusion. She did not argue though. Instead, she walked past him and up the stairs to their room, where he told her to sit on the bed for a moment and headed into their bathroom. A moment later she heard the tub filling.

She spent half an hour lounging in the warm bubble bath he'd drawn for her. He washed her hair for her, massaging her scalp as he did so. Then he combed her hair and dressed her in the silk nightgown he'd bought on his way home from work that evening.

When she was again clothed, he laid her in their bed and sat with her. She reveled in his aftercare with his loving arms around her and her bottom still stinging from the lashing he had given her.

An evening spent with him in such a way always left her exhausted and fulfilled. The force of his slaps and the passion in his kisses mingled together to bring her to new heights each time they played. She was thankful they had found this new life together, traveling down the same road.

Sleep came easy to her with him by her side, and she dreamt of new delicious tortures he might come up with for their next date together.

Freedom Chain

The instructor did not allow Ryanna to finish her dance. He halted her performance halfway through.

"Your strides are too great! Your feet should be closer together so as not to look clumsy. Ballerinas should be graceful, like a leaf falling gently down from a tree in the fall," he chastised her.

Ryanna remained still while he, a much sought after dance instructor, walked around her deep in thought. She felt naked when he peered at her in such a way.

"I have it!" he declared and disappeared into the storage closet. He returned holding a pair of leather anklets.

She stood silently in awe as he locked each leather strap. Once the chain was secured, linking her ankles together, he stood and smiled.

"There! Now again!" He clapped his hands, and the music began to play.

The leather restraints were tight around her ankles, almost painfully so. She looked at her instructor with new eyes.

Fantasy No. 1

Candles burned brightly, lighting the room to create a soft glow—every size and shape candle available at the local stores: fat, short, long, square, oval, circular, all lit perfectly on the table tops and along the ledges of the northern wall.

Were it not for the small window in the room, where the moon's light spilled through, there would be no outside distraction from the beauty of the dancing flames. The walls of the small room in the far corner of the southern ranch were decorated with oil paintings; some bought at the local flea markets and others painted by the woman of the house. The scenes, though similar in genre, all took on individual warmth and emotion.

A particular favorite one of the couple was of a woman kneeling on a cobblestone street, her hands stretched over her head holding out a gift to the man who stood before her. In her hands a small box, what the box held was left up to the admirer's imagination.

The woman of the house liked to believe the box held the woman's heart, an offering to her lover. The man of the dwelling believed inside the box lay the woman's soul, her power, and her submission.

The silence of the room was broken by the jingling of a metal chain brushing up against the hard floor. The man, Lucien, sitting at a desk in the far off corner of the room, glanced upward toward the noise. He smiled as he saw his lady standing barefoot, her hands held over her head by a chain that connected to the ceiling, her feet bound together by yet another chain, leather cuffs around her ankles.

"Did you wish to speak?" he asked, pushing his chair back to turn toward his toy, his lover. The scraping of the wood against the floor echoed throughout the room. He cocked his head, as though he were awaiting her to speak, and laughed when he looked at her mouth. A wooden bit was being clenched nicely between her teeth, a well-crafted piece of work he had bought at the local ranch, too big for a baby mare but too small for a full grown horse. Perfect for his lady's mouth.

"Kara, If you wish to speak, tap your foot three times." He spoke to her from across the room. He looked down at her bare feet and watched as she slowly, with some difficulty due to the restraints, tapped her foot on the floor three times.

He laughed with delight as he stood from his chair. "I had requested silence before…so that I might get some work done." He spoke as he made his way across the room. "You didn't seem fit to obey that simple request. Shall I grant you yours?" He paused a few steps away from her, admiring her breasts. Her nipples were erect, her breasts round and itching to be touched, to be suckled, to be whipped. His lips thinned into a stretched grin.

"Shall I? Two taps for yes and three for no." He gestured to her feet. He heard her moan and saw her pulling on the chains. This was difficult for her, to be chained in such a way, to be gazed upon, treated as an object for his enjoyment. He was proud of her for enduring it for him.

"Well, should I let you speak?" he asked again.

Kara tried to convey her plea with her eyes. The cuffs on her wrists were starting to bite into her skin. He hadn't chosen the fur lined cuffs like she had hoped, but rather he'd decided on the cold metal rings.

She hadn't meant to disturb his work; she knew the importance of his upcoming morning meeting. She meant only to see what he wanted for dinner. When he had first put her into her cuffs and placed the gag in her mouth, she had thought he was displeased with her. But now seeing the enjoyment he was having, she knew he was looking for some fun.

"Are you listening to me?" Lucien questioned harshly, pulling her back with his tone to his strength, his unwavering dominance.

She lightly tapped her foot two times, feeling her cheeks burn from the embarrassment of having to communicate in such a way.

"Do you believe I should let you speak?" He reached his hand out to pinch her taut nipple.

She squealed at the sensation of his touch, the pain of his fingers, and the tingle it left behind. She tapped her foot two times.

"You do."

Slowly he walked around her, plucking a crop from the wall as he passed. "Well," he mused, tapping the crop against her buttocks lightly at first and then harder until she wiggled from the sting. "I enjoy you silent like this, bound helplessly, hanging in front of me," he admitted.

Lucien continued to tap the crop against her bare skin as he circled her once more, the way she wiggled to avoid the crop pleased him. If he were younger, he might have been nervous from the excitement she caused. "I guess it's a good thing that you don't make these decisions." He chuckled as he kissed her cheek. Her skin reminded him of satin bedding. The lotions she continuously cluttered the bathroom with worked well.

She moaned loudly and pulled on the chains harder. Her show of frustration fueled him. She fought the sensations he raised in her, fighting with her inner self that told her she should not be treated in such a way. She was becoming rebellious. He loved her this way. The taming was more enjoyable than the catch, he always thought.

Stepping back again, he looked at her, lifting her breast with his right hand and holding it up further than she would have allowed were her hands not bound. Using his left hand, he assaulted her nipple with the crop. Her squeals brought delight to his heart; a warmth covered him as she began to dance from the pleasure he was causing her.

Lucien dropped her breast and crouched down before her. Using the crop, he slapped her inner thighs, then lightly spanked her swollen, wet clit.

"You do enjoy this, don't you, my little toy?" He stood and pushed his finger into her and began to rub her clit with his palm. "Don't you?" he asked with an evil grin.

She moaned loudly as the crop crashed down on her bottom, and he drove his finger into her again.

"Answer," he commanded and looked down at her feet.

He heard the groan, the muffled sigh, the determination not to answer with her feet. He looked at her face, admired the redness in her cheeks, the unshed tears of passion, the delightful smile under her gag. He slapped her bottom harder.

She grunted and reluctantly tapped her foot twice.

"Good girl," he cooed in her ear as he removed his finger. He ran the crop over her skin as he shifted his position around her.

"I love the sight of your ass." He admired her as he slapped her cheeks. He adored the way her ass bounced after each slap of the crop.

He hung the crop back on its proper nail and went to the latch that held her ropes. He felt her eyes on him as he loosened the rope only to drag her forward until she was bent over, and again, he tightened the hold they had on her.

The position gave him full access and a view of all of her fun parts. He was glad for deciding against giving her the spanking bench to lean over. Having her displayed like this was better for them both.

"There, that's better, don't you think?" he asked, rubbing her ass as she stared at the floor.

She shook her head and received a prompt, harshly placed slap to her bottom. She moaned and tapped her foot twice.

He moved again to stand behind her and let his hands wander over her smooth skin. There were no traces of the whipping she had received a week ago. He positioned his hands between her legs, felt her wetness and grinned. He slid his hands still further and gripped both her nipples. He heard her squeal, her moan, her thrill as he pulled hard on them, twisting them downward. Her muscles tightened beneath him.

Before she could adjust to the pain in her breasts, he let go. He waited for the second rush of sensations to wash over her before leaving her.

He opened several drawers, allowing her to hear the scrape of the wood and wonder what he could be searching for.

Being bent over in such a way left her completely exposed to him, to his eyes, to his lust, to whatever he chose. He loved her this way.

Emotions flitted through her expression. He could see her worry about his plans and also her giddiness at the prospect of the fun he had planned.

He slipped his finger between her ass cheeks and rubbed cool lotion over her tight hole. Keeping her spread open with one hand, he slipped the plug into her.

She cried out from the invasion.

Lucien held her hips, massaging her until the burning subsided and only the fullness of the plug remained.

"Now you look the part." He patted her back. "Look." He pushed her head down for her to see the long hair-like material of the tail hanging between her legs.

He wondered if she recalled him looking with a wanting smile at the pony plugs during a recent shopping excursion to his favorite toy shop.

He noticed tears pooling in her eyes. This was utter humiliation for her. His already hard dick pushed against the restraint of his pants. Tears and cries only amplified his lust.

"Are you comfy?" he asked, patting her rear again. She shook her head.

"I'm sorry?" he asked with a harder swat to her ass. She tapped her foot three times.

"No? Are the binds too tight?" he questioned.

Three taps of her foot.

"Is the plug too big?" he asked, pushing on it a bit, smiling over the grunt he heard.

Three more taps.

"No? Then what's wrong?" He pushed the plug harder and delighted in the wiggle of her ass when he touched her.

"Are you aware you are mine to do with as I wish?" He looked down at her feet, two taps.

He pulled a paddle from a hook on the wall. The long wooden one she'd enjoyed so much only a few nights prior.

"You know you belong to me, completely, and I would not harm you…in a bad way, that is." He petted her hair.

Two taps.

"And you trust me?"

Two taps.

24

"Then what could be bothering you?" He mused playfully. "Is it that you are helpless? That you can't do anything but bend over in such a way that your entire body is at my disposal. That I can fuck you if I want, and spank you if I want." He added a solid swat to her ass with the paddle for emphasis.

Her moan, displaying her frustration of simultaneous pleasure and humiliation, was a gift he savored.

"Is it the humiliation you are feeling?" he asked.

Two taps of her foot, he nodded.

"Well, being humbled isn't a bad thing. Especially for a rebellious girl like you," he answered with another swat of the paddle.

Kara felt the plug push harder as he spanked her, and she tried to move away from him, away from the punishing pleasure that overwhelmed her.

"Instead of fighting your feelings, instead of betraying yourself, why do you not accept who you are? Feel what you feel and enjoy it?" he asked as he slapped her again with the paddle.

She lost time during the spanking. Her bottom glowed deep red from the game he played. The more she danced to avoid the paddle, the more direct his aim at the plug. Suddenly, the paddle was gone, the heat of her bottom still proof it had been there.

He moved to stand beside her.

The room filled with the hum of a vibrator. Lucien dragged it down her back. Her shoulders relaxed when he touched her clit with it, and she moaned loudly when he slapped her lightly with it.

"Don't fight. Just feel." His voice was hot against her ear as he whispered and ran the vibrator over her clit hard, unyielding.

She could feel her thighs tighten, knew she was close. He reached under her and began to twist her nipples again, pushing harder bring her to her climax.

She moved against the vibrator, trying to fuck it, trying to come.

"Do you want to come?" He removed the toy from her reach.

There was no hesitation now, she tapped her foot hard two times.

"Good girl." Lucien kissed her and placed the magic wand against her clit. He listened to the chains move as she fucked it. He felt the muscles in her legs tense, heard her scream out as the waves hit her. He locked eyes with her when she began to scream louder as she ended her orgasm.

He turned the vibrator off, went back to the table, and placed it down, looking at her now bent over with the pony plug, her chest rising and falling rapidly as she tried to regain her breath. He was filled with joy and pride.

He went to the pulley and brought her back to standing. His gaze lingered on her breasts heaving from her rapid breath. He undid her cuffs in silence and gently brought her hands down to her side, rubbing her arms lightly.

She stared up at him, looking into his eyes.

Swiftly, he undid her ankle cuffs and rubbed away the soreness before standing.

"Stay." A simple command. Her eyes were on him as he made his way back to his desk. He casually sat in his chair and smiled at her.

"Kneel," he commanded with a small gesture of his hand.

Without hesitation, she moved to her knees.

"Crawl to me." His demand was softened by the erotic grin dancing on his lips.

She crawled slowly to him, wiggling her hips as she did so, caressing him with her eyes as she moved closer to him. When she got to his feet, she bent lower and placed her lips on his boot.

He was pleased at her attempt to obey their protocol, even with her lips parted from the gag, and he patted her head.

"Up." He pulled on her collar until she knelt again. He untied the leather straps and removed the bit from her mouth.

She moved her lips a bit and licked at them. She looked up at him, watched him unzip his pants, and smiled at the sight of his cock being brought out.

"Do you need further command?" he asked slyly.

Kara shook her head and bent over, keeping her ass high in the air, the pony plug still in place. She was hungry for him, for the taste of him, for the feel of his cock against her tongue, between her teeth. She kept her hands on his thighs as she did her mystical dance with her mouth.

She enjoyed his moans, yearned for his sighs, and longed to feel his hot cum on her tongue. The words "good girl" warmed her soul. She prepared herself, lapping at his balls, sucking on his dick, she felt him tighten, and she sat still as he exploded.

His cum hit the back of her throat, and she hungrily swallowed. She licked him clean and looked up at him with a smile on her lips.

He looked down at her, his pleasure evident in his gaze as he ran his fingers through her hair. He stood and clipped the linking chain leash to her collar.

She crawled proudly by his side as he led her to the small cot in the corner of the room. She knelt over the side of the bed for him to remove the plug, and he rewarded her with a few more swats of his hand.

Tucking her into the cot, he sat beside her and ran his finger down her cheek. "I'm proud of you." His words were like silk wrapping around her body.

"I have to work now. Sleep." He kissed her on the tip of her nose and then on her lips.

He left her to return to his work, not bothering to look back.

She watched him for a moment, admiring the strength in his walk, the confidence in his stance.

Once he was at his desk, deep in his thoughts, she let her heavy lids close and drifted to sleep.

The Carry On

Sunlight streamed into the dank hotel room. Bed sheets freshly pressed made for an inviting place to catch a nap while waiting.

The long trip left the obedient companion drowsy, her lids fell over her eyes, whisking her away to slumber.

The sleeping visitor was nestled cozily where her Master had packed her. Her long, silky legs nuzzled against her naked breasts, and her hands were tucked neatly under her chin as she slept.

He'd promised the meeting would be short. He would be returning to unpack his bag any moment.

The far off sound of a vacuum running roused the sleeping woman. A quick glance around the room told her he had not returned. How she longed to stretch her legs and wrap them around him…

Fantasy No. 2

The floor felt cold against her warm skin. Her joints ached from kneeling for such a long time. She had been in her position with her back as straight as the posture bar would allow for much longer than she'd originally anticipated.

She suddenly wished she had used the washroom before coming down to his den. She squirmed, trying to relieve the pressure on her bladder.

The sound of a chair scraping against the stone floor enveloped her, and she held her breath as she heard him move around. The thick black fabric tied behind her head, covering her eyes, acted as a safety blanket for her. She didn't trust herself that she would be able to keep from watching his every move if her eyes weren't blindfolded.

She loved to watch her Master move about his den. He walked with such purpose and confidence in his stride; every step he took aroused her.

"Our guests are here." She heard his cheerful voice as he walked to the back door, opening it.

Several footsteps entered the room. A gentle woman's voice greeted him. Then a command was given in a harsh tone that she did not understand.

She held her breath as the footsteps moved closer to her. She could feel them near her, looking at her. She tried to sit straighter, to look proud. She felt a long fingernail lift her nipple, and she gasped at the touch.

"Nicely endowed," the woman said in a flat tone.

Merely a fact stated and not a compliment given. The scent of lavender perfume filled the air as the woman walked around the kneeling slave. "Is her ass as firm as it looks?" There was a hint of disappointment in her voice.

"She does have a tight ass, but it bounces well enough against the paddles and crops. The whips leave nice marks too." Her Master spoke with pride, pride for her.

"This gag, can we remove it or is she being punished?" The woman pushed a finger against the ball the slave held firmly between her teeth.

"She isn't being punished at the moment. If you would like to remove, it you may," he answered.

The slave could feel her Master standing before her; she could almost picture his stance—tall, dominating the room with his arms folded over his chest, almost a bored look in his eyes.

"No, I think I like her this way. Silent. I have heard too much chatter from my own slave this morning." The woman sounded amused. "I wish I could stay for the fun, but I do have to run off. I should be back by morning. I appreciate you taking care of Vanessa for me; she can be a handful, but I'm sure you can handle that." The woman's smile reached her voice.

The slave wished she could see the woman's face. She pictured her having soft features, dark blue eyes, and tightly tied back blonde hair.

"Not a problem. Anything I should know?" She heard her Master ask as they walked from her, leaving her kneeling on the floor, her legs spread, her mouth gagged.

She wished she could see the slave the Mistress had left in her Master's care.

"Not really. You know her well enough, she has no allergies or anything medical that she needs tending to. I should be back by morning, if I'm delayed I will be sure to give you a call." The Mistress spoke softly. The sound of a gentle kiss echoed in the silent room, and the door shut.

"Vanessa, stand," her Master commanded of the visiting slave. "I do not allow my slaves to be dressed while in this room, remove your clothing," he stated and walked across the room.

She perked up at the gentle touch of his fingertips on her forehead and whimpered softly as her Master fondled her nipples, rubbing them, pulling at them. His warm breath blanketed her neck as he kissed her softly.

"We are going to have a lot of fun today." He cooed in her ear. "Vanessa, come here." His voice was stern and hot. "Kneel facing her," he commanded the second slave.

The slave could feel Vanessa only a hair's breath from herself. Her Master moved from her side, and she was surprised by a pinch on her nipple. She groaned from the shock of it.

Suddenly, the blindfold was pulled free from her eyes, and she squinted as the light shined into them.

"Vanessa you remember my slave?" he asked.

She watched as her Master pulled on Vanessa's nipple hard.

"Yes," the new slave cried out. "Yes, Sir," she quickly amended when he applied more pressure to her nipple.

"Your Mistress left me with a few suggestions for you today." There was a wickedness in his smile. "Stand," he directed as he pulled her up, still holding onto her nipple. Without releasing her, she was walked across the room to the cross he'd recently installed.

He took her arms and pulled them over her head, chaining each hand to the top of the cross. He smiled down at her as he did so. Next, he bent and chained each foot to the bottom of the cross, leaving her immobile, vertical. He patted her left cheek and turned to attend to his own slave.

She watched him walk toward her with determination in his eyes. She thought he would unclasp the bar behind her, to free her hands. She was wrong.

He merely bent over and picked her up; she kept her position as best as she could as he carried her to the cross. He placed her down in front of the chained slave, her face near the woman's crotch.

She could smell the other slave's sex, her wetness, and she smiled through her gag.

Her Master slowly unclasped the gag, and removed it from her mouth. He looked upon her with pride and expectation. There was more longing in her than she could describe or admit.

He pushed her chin until she was once again facing Vanessa. "Open your mouth," he commanded in a soft tone, and she obeyed with unwavering submission.

He pushed the back of her head until her mouth rested directly over Vanessa's cunt. He smiled devilishly when he heard both slaves moan in unison. He looked at them for a moment and shook his head. Without speaking to either, he acted quickly to remove the cuff's from Vanessa's feet and spread them further apart.

When he appeared to be satisfied and she was sufficiently open, he re-cuffed her and went back to his slave. She had not moved; she had been utterly obedient. He patted her shoulder, a known signal that she was doing well in his eyes.

"Lean back for a moment." He pulled on his slave's ponytail, her hair up the way he liked it when she was in her collar. "Now lick her clit." He gave his direction, keeping a hold on her hair.

She bit her lip a second then discretely put her tongue out and licked Vanessa's clit. She blushed considerably and pulled away. She was rewarded with a hard yank on her hair. She cried out from the sting in her scalp.

"No. Lap her clit like a dog would lap a bowl of water… Would you care to practice with the water first?" he asked, knowing she found that particular ritual to be humiliating.

"No, Master." A plea.

"Oh? Then do as I say, the first time I say it." He chastised her. "Now lick her clit." He shoved her head into Vanessa's crotch again.

She again put her tongue out and quickly began licking at the clit before her. She tasted the wetness, felt the slickness of the cunt before her. She licked faster, hungrily, the way she knew he wanted. She turned her head slightly and licked the lips, licked the juices from the slave before her. It was a humiliation to service another slave with her hands bound behind her, her master holding her head in place.

Her own arousal began to drip onto her thighs.

She could hear the moans coming from Vanessa, could feel the woman's thighs tighten against her cheeks, she hoped Vanessa wouldn't come. She couldn't bear to have to eat the cum of another slave. Surely, if Vanessa did not gain permission before doing so, she would also receive punishment for bringing the slave to orgasm.

Vanessa, do not come, she thought to herself…*do not come.* She urged in her mind.

"Vanessa likes to moan." She heard the delight in her Master's tone. He was enjoying the scene before him. "I think I will keep her without a gag… Her moans have an effect on you," he said to his slave, reaching a hand down and dipping his finger into her sex.

She groaned at the fiery pleasure of his finger. She felt his grasp loosen and leave her hair. She was no longer being held under the woman's cunt. She willingly licked at her clit, eating her pussy, licking up her juices. She blushed horribly at the sight she must be to her Master.

She sensed her Master leaving her, felt his absence as he walked away from the pair. He was standing behind her now, watching. She imagined his grin of enjoyment at the sight her and her playmate.

"Faster." He nudged her ass with his booted foot.

She moved her tongue quickly around the clit, lapping at it intensely, with fury, as she felt his foot nudge her again. She continued on as her tongue became tired; she sucked on the lips, moving her head side to side using her own lips to bring enjoyment to the slave bound before her.

"Did I say to do that?" he asked with a slap of his hand across her ass.

She jumped at the unexpected sting.

"Did I say to eat her…no…I said to lick her." He sounded displeased.

Her heart sank.

She didn't stop in her movement, but instead began to lick again furiously at the clit. She felt his hand reach under her chin, heard the snap of the leash being put on her collar. She moaned inwardly.

"Come," he directed, yanking on her leash, pulling her from her task.

She followed him, walking on her knees, cursing herself for her actions. He lead her to a cage that sat in the corner of the room, beside his work desk. She moaned when she saw him walk toward it.

"Stay," he commanded with a yank on the chain; she remained still.

She watched as he left the room for a moment and went into the small kitchen. When he returned, she wanted to cry.

He carried a bowl, a large dog bowl, with the word "Slave" written on it. He walked back to her and placed the bowl inside the cage, which was large enough for her to crawl into and turn around, big enough for her to sit comfortably for hours. She hated the cage almost as much as the bowl.

He crouched behind his slave, undid her wrists, and pulled the posture bar from her collar. She shook her hands a bit to get the blood flowing properly again, but before she could rub them properly, she heard his command.

"In." Simple. To the point. No mistake as to what he was referring to.

She looked quickly up at him begging him, a silent plea for him not to make her.

He knew this was hard for her. Another slave was watching, enjoying this scene. She was being pushed, and he was not going to let her push back.

"In…or do you need a whipping to get you going?" he questioned with a raised eyebrow.

She shook her head and knelt on all fours, waiting for him to unleash her. He removed the leash from her collar and spanked her ass as she rushed into the cage.

She crawled in and turned around, so she was now facing him. She watched as he closed the door and locked it, taking the key and putting it in his pocket.

"Drink." He pointed to the water bowl.

She hesitated, feeling the tears puddle in her eyes, and the heat rush to her cheeks.

She glanced momentarily at Vanessa, hanging on the cross, smiling a wicked smile. She felt the tears fall down her cheeks as she bent over further, letting her tongue dip into the water.

"Good girl." She heard her Master speak gently. "Keep practicing." He left her in her cage, drinking water.

She watched from her bowl as he walked to Vanessa and felt the tears spill more rapidly.

He unlocked the other slave's cuffs and helped her to step away from the cross. He hooked a finger through the loop in the thin leather collar she wore around her neck and walked her to the bench.

Instructing her to lay across it, he stepped away to observe as she gracefully laid with her back pressed firmly to the wood. Reaching above him, he pulled down the small rings that hung there.

He secured each of her feet to one of the rings and went to the wall to pull them back up into the air. He watched as her feet were pulled up; he stopped only when her ass was fully in view, her sex glistening in the light. He smiled.

Taking her hands, he pulled them over her head. He cuffed her wrists together and brought down another ring, locking her into place. He stepped back to admire her.

Her muscular legs were spread high in the air, and her hands were bound above her, effectively raising her breasts and stretching her torso. She was a beautiful sight.

He looked back at the cage and watched his own slave lapping water from her bowl, and his lips curved with pleasure from her obedience.

She tried to keep herself focused on her task, but her Master's smile brought warmth to her heart, and she could not resist the grin that crossed her lips.

The Master walked away from Vanessa and went to a cabinet. She heard the wrangling sounds of toys being gathered. When he returned, he ran a finger over the breasts of the bound slave, took her wanting nipple between his fingers and squeezed. He appeared delighted in the squeal he was rewarded with.

He wasted no time in pinching the second nipple;

again, she writhed from the sensation. He picked up the clamps he had retrieved and was quick about placing them on her.

Once each nipple was properly clamped, he put his finger under the small chain that linked them together and pulled upward.

"Oh, that sound. The squeak of my toys reminds me of my years as a musician. The perfectly tuned instrument can bring about so many emotions." He sounded distant, as though he was speaking to himself and not the plaything before him. He pulled once again to hear the yelp of the slave, much like a violinist plucks at the tight strings of his instrument.

He looked down at her cunt. "Your Mistress doesn't keep you bare," he noted aloud. "That's interesting. She keeps her own pussy naked of all hair. I wonder if she does that to indulge you."

Vanessa swallowed but did not respond.

He trailed a thin, wooden stick along her right leg, starting at her foot and ending at her pussy. He grinned when she sucked in her breath.

She had played this game before; she knew what was coming.

He held the bottom of the stick firmly with one hand and used the other to pull the top of it back. He let loose and watched it slap against her inner thigh. She could tell the soft red mark it left behind pleased him as well as the sound of the tormented slave. He again flicked the wooden rod against the slave's thigh, switching to her left leg, then returning to her right.

She squirmed in her restraints, crying out, shrieking with each new strike of the rod. Anyone outside of the room listening would believe the slave was being cruelly tortured, instead of being beautifully pleasured.

He leaned closer to look at her pussy, using his fingers to pry open the lips. He rubbed her clit momentarily, hearing her pleas for more, when he pulled his finger away from her. The finger was replaced with the small rod; he flicked the sides of her lips, hitting the tender area between her pussy and her leg.

He almost chuckled when she began to scream out. He continued his torture, switching from one side to the next, moving to her thighs and back to her pussy.

He listened to her yells, her squeals, her moans. He smiled sweetly when she sucked in her breath, and he gave an evil grin when she tried to move away from him. He stood above her and reached over to pull on her nipple chain. Her yelp fell softly onto his ears.

He reached to the side of her, where he had laid his weapons and pulled the cane to him. He slid it under the small chain and raised it until her nipples were being pulled upward, and she cried out from the sensation. The cane was withdrawn, and he stepped to the side, looking at her breasts.

"Your tits are almost as big as my slave's," he commented dryly, tapping the cane against her breasts.

She looked at him. She was not gagged, but she remained silent, breathing steadily, biting at her lips as he intensified the taps.

He moved his concentration to her ass. He held the cane against her cheeks and looked into her eyes as he brought it back and unleashed it on her. He watched her lids open wide in shock, her lips parted to scream silently. He continued in this manner for a few moments, letting her writhe beneath the punishing pleasure of his cane.

When he was satisfied with his work, he raked his hands over the small welts forming on her ass and dropped the cane to the floor. He ran his finger through her pussy lips again.

"Are you horny?" he asked the slave, who looked at him with desperation. "Are you?" he asked again, pinching her clit.

"Yes, Sir," she called out, clenching her eyes shut.

"Do you want to be fucked?" he asked, again pinching her.

"Yes, Sir," she nearly screamed.

He released her clit, left her on the bench in silence, and walked to the cage where his slave had witnessed the entire scene.

His slave knelt in the cage, the bowl before her empty. Her eyes full of lust and craving. The scene before her had worked her libido into a frenzy that only he knew how to tame.

He unlocked the door, pushing it open, and hung her leash in front of the opening. A silent command for her to crawl out. She obeyed, thankful for the escape of the cruel bars of the cage.

He clipped her leash back onto her collar and walked her to the bench where Vanessa lay with her legs spread. He pulled on the collar, stopping his slave, and gave her the command to kneel.

She knelt with her shoulders back, her chest out, and her hands resting on her open knees.

She could hear him walking around but did not dare to turn her head to see what he was doing. When he returned, he began to pet her, to run his fingers over her chin. She pushed her cheek into his hand.

"Open," he commanded gently as he tapped his finger on her lips.

She parted her lips wide, expecting the ball gag to be put back in place. She was surprised when she saw the dildo for a second before it was strapped into her mouth. She wrapped her lips around the small ball that rested on her tongue and looked downward at the cock protruding outward. She felt the tears swell in her eyes again, and she looked at him with pleading.

"This is no worse than the ball gag." He comforted

her with a pat on her head. Then he went to the wall and loosened the ropes that held Vanessa's legs. He brought them down slightly so her cunt lowered, and he retightened the rope.

"This slave wishes to be fucked." He knelt beside his slave. "So you will fuck her." He pushed aside a stray hair from her cheek with his finger. His smile held confidence and comfort. He helped her lean forward and placed the dildo at the tip of the Vanessa's neatly trimmed cunt. He sat back on his heels and pinched his slave's nipples to get her to move.

She was quick in her thrust, watching the dildo slide into Vanessa. She heard the other slave moan.

She pulled back slightly and pushed forward again. She continued in this manner, finding it somewhat difficult to maneuver the dildo in such a fashion. She bit down on the ball inside her mouth, feeling her cheeks burning with embarrassment.

"Put your ass in the air." His firm voice broke into her concentration.

She stilled her movements and slowly repositioned herself, pushing her ass up as far as she could. She felt his fingers probing her, pushing into her, fondling her. She moaned her own pleasure as she pushed the dildo again into the slave before her.

She felt the vibrations against her clit, and she could hear her own vibrator being used. She writhed against the toy, shaking her ass in the manner he found so delightful.

She did not stop fucking Vanessa out of fear he would stop playing with her if she did.

She listened to the sounds of the slave before her, feeling the vibrations on her on clit, and she moaned loudly as she continued. She knew he was watching, knew he was smiling. She fucked the slave faster, harder.

"Move back for a moment." He pulled on his slave's hair, freeing her from the other slave's cunt. With one hand, he managed to unstrap the dildo gag and drop it to the floor.

"Now eat her, lick her, eat her, make her come. Eat every drop of it," he instructed her.

She felt the vibrator move away from her clit and quickly put her mouth on Vanessa's arousal.

She licked hard, running her tongue over the clit, over the lips, then dipping into the other woman's cunt.

She sucked on the lips, swallowing the juices that she captured with her tongue.

"You may use your fingers if you wish."

She quickly pushed her finger into Vanessa, smiling at the peaceful yelp she heard. She began to finger-fuck the slave with vigor and lick at her clit.

Faster and harder she pressed her tongue against it, lapping at it, enjoying herself. She felt the vibrator, and she moved her own hips against it.

She felt Vanessa's thighs tighten, moving slightly when she thrust her hips upward. The other slave was close; she knew it.

She flicked her tongue rapidly over the slave's cunt, devouring her, fingering her faster.

"Come." She heard her Master's order to Vanessa, and she braced herself.

She flicked her tongue as fast as she could, and was rewarded with a scream of ecstasy. She could feel the tension in Vanessa's upcoming release.

She removed her finger and replaced it with her tongue. Using it to fuck the slave, she put her slick fingers to work rubbing the other slave's clit.

She felt the explosion, felt the hot cum leak onto her tongue. She removed her hand and went to the task of licking the slave clean as Vanessa began to calm.

She kept her tongue in place until her Master pulled

on her hair to bring her back.

He removed the vibrator and stood, moving her to her feet. He kept his grasp on her hair as he walked her to where Vanessa's head lay.

The slave had a smile on her face, a peaceful expression.

"Stand over her," he instructed his slave.

She lifted her leg and took a step, placing Vanessa between her thighs.

Master put his lips near Vanessa's ear. "Now, eat my slave, eat her as good as she ate you." He gave his command and stood against the wall to watch and admire.

He knew his slave would want him to touch her, to play with her breasts, but he wouldn't. She had to learn she was his to command, and he would give when he wanted to give.

He watched Vanessa stick her tongue upward, lapping at his slave as best as her position would allow. He enjoyed seeing his slave rub her clit against Vanessa's mouth, Vanessa's tongue fucking her.

He knew she was close; he saw it in her eyes. He kept his gaze locked on her as she moaned and squealed.

"Master! May I come!?" she asked as she continued to move faster on Vanessa, her chest heaving with the deep, fast breaths she took.

"Yes, you may." His breath caught at the scene before him. She ground her hips quickly, and he listened as she screamed her orgasm when Vanessa's tongue dove into his slave's cunt. He smiled with pleasure when he saw his slave's shoulders slump. She was exhausted.

He walked over to her, kissed her deeply and looked into her eyes. "I'm proud of you," he whispered as he helped her step over the slave and stand at her side. "Stay here a moment," he instructed.

He untied Vanessa, freed her of her nipple clamps,

and rubbed her breasts, before helping her to stand. He walked her to the small cot he had placed in the corner of the room and instructed her to rest, patting her head.

He walked back to his slave and kissed her again. "You did well. I know it was hard for you, but do you understand?" he asked her.

She looked puzzled.

"Do you understand you do what pleases me? If pleasing another slave does that, then you will do so."

"Yes, Master," she whispered, feeling her cheeks burn again.

"I do love it when you blush." His laughter was soft. "And if I were to instruct you to please her Mistress when she arrives in the morning?"

"Then I will do so, Master," she answered swiftly.

"Good girl. You need to rest. I've pushed you further than I have in the past. But first, I will bathe you. Go upstairs and fill the tub," he instructed and sent her on her way with a pat to her rear.

He walked to Vanessa after his slave had gone up to do his bidding. He sat next to her on the cot and ran his hands over her breasts.

"Are you sore?" he asked her.

"A little, Sir," she answered meekly.

"Your Mistress will be very proud of you." He smiled at her.

"Thank you, Sir."

"Rest now. We will be going out for dinner tonight." He smiled devilishly. "You will need your strength." He tweaked her nipple before standing and going to attend his slave.

His obedient, caring, loving slave.

He sighed with pleasure as he walked up the stairs. She made him proud; she exceeded any expectations he'd had for her.

He smiled again to himself as he opened the door to

the washroom and found her standing in the tub awaiting him…

For the Taking

Blindfold in place, Cassie listened intently to pinpoint his location. Her collar felt heavy around her neck. The leather restraints of the table imprisoned her hands perfectly, as well as her feet. The position kept her open for him.

Unexpectedly, she felt his warm breath over her wetness, and she bit down on her lip.

She stiffened against the restraints as a single fingertip traced her flesh.

"You hate to love this," he whispered against her sex.

The restraints held fast to her as she bucked against them when his tongue gently brushed her hungry clit.

"And I love that you hate it."

Verbal Bondage

The chill in the air wrapped around her as though to blanket her from the warmth. The dampness seeped into her bare flesh as she sat quietly in the corner. She could turn the heater on. It was only a step or two from where she sat, but she dared not move from her seat.

She raised her eyes from the floor and looked at the metal rings cemented permanently to the walls. Chains dangled from them with a lifelessness that held promise. The realization that she was not to be restrained with the chains had been a comfort.

She'd felt grateful when he'd told her to straddle the straight back chair and stare at the wall. She would be free from the unforgiving, cold, biting metal cuffs. Only a verbal command kept her in place.

Being chained in place would be too easy for her, she soon realized. There would be no choice to make with the cuffs in place. She would stay put because the chains made her do so. But freedom from the physical bondage gave her a choice. Obey or disobey.

She thought her chastisement lenient, having done what she did, to merely have to sit in the corner like a naughty school girl. It gave her a bit of a thrill when he had given his command.

The silence of the room made her head ache. She wished he'd come back for her, forgive her disobedience, and hold her in his arms.

She fidgeted on the wooden chair, trying to find a comfortable position. The wood scratched at her bare

skin, as though she sat on sandpaper. The last time she'd
sat on the uncomfortable seat was after a long whipping
with his belt. The current discomfort proved easily
tolerable in comparison.

He'd brought her down to their private room, the
only room of the house which visitors and friends would
never enter—did not even know existed.

Being led by her collar and leash to the center of the
room was at times a prelude to a wonderful flogging
session, not this time, however. He'd removed the leash
from the thick metal ring that dangled from the center of
her black leather collar. He'd stepped back and basked in
the beauty of the woman before him. Even when she'd
been disobedient, she saw passion and lust in his eyes.

She'd stood with her hands folded in front of her,
with her fingers gripping onto the skirt of her sundress,
as though it could shield her from his displeasure. She'd
looked at him with worry and remorse.

She had known he would find the toy, knew it the
moment she'd remembered leaving it out on the dresser.
He would find it, and he would know she'd taken
advantage of his absence for the morning.

He'd dropped her leash onto the small wooden
table, the clanking of the metal interlocking chains of the
leash echoing in the room.

If someone were to wander into their room, they
would be shocked to see the array of devices on the
table. Different sized leashes, a metal collar, several
paddles, and a coil of rope laid methodically out for
future use. If they were to open the closet door a few feet
away from the table, they would be surprised to find
whips, floggers of many colors and sizes, and more
paddles hanging and waiting for their turn to be used.

"Have you given yourself to me?" His voice, steady
and strong broke the silence.

"Yes, Sir," she answered in a hushed tone, keeping

her gaze on his chest, afraid to look into his eyes and see the disappointment there.

"You've given your heart, your mind, and your body to me?" He picked up a small paddle from the table and caressed the black worn leather with his fingers.

"Yes, Sir." She shifted her eyes to the paddle and felt herself clench at the sight of it.

He placed the paddle down and picked up the short bullwhip he'd recently acquired. Her breath caught in her throat and she knew she would learn much from that whip were he to use it.

"If your body belongs to me, they why did you see fit to touch it without me present or without my consent?" He moved his gaze from the whip in his hands to her eyes.

She stared at the weapon he held and swallowed hard.

"Well?" he asked with more heat.

"I-I don't know," she answered sluggishly with a drop in her posture. She wished there had been a reasonable explanation as to why she had not waited for him to return or did not call him on his cell. Something that would allow him to rein in his disappointment, but she knew there could be nothing she offered that would lessen the offense.

He dropped the whip back onto the table, and her relief made it easier to fill her lungs. Then he walked to her, around her, looking down at her.

She remained still, not moving a muscle, breathing deeply, unsure of what was to happen next. She disliked the not knowing part of these moments, and he used the information wisely.

"Put your hands over your head," he commanded, standing behind her.

With her arms raised over her head, she heard movement behind her, but she did not take the chance of turning her head. She felt a cold, sharp metal shaft at the base of her neck and sucked in a breath. Before the first snip, she knew what he was doing.

She shuddered as he used the scissors to cut away her sun dress, her favorite. Each snip of the shears cut through her with guilt of her disobedience. She felt tears in her eyes as the cool air hit her bare back; she took slow breaths as he cut through the cotton fabric of her sleeves. She wanted to cry out, to look at the damage he had done and see if she could mend the dress. She closed her eyes when he ripped the torn garment from her body, leaving her naked to his eyes.

She felt vulnerable, standing with her arms over her head, exposed to him, open to his judgment and pleasure. She cautiously opened her eyes to see him standing in front of her.

He sized her up, as though he were buying a prized ham and wanted to make sure it was worthy of the price.

She looked to the floor, not wanting to bear witness to her own humiliation. He positioned himself closer until the tips of his boots touched the tips of her bare feet.

"This belongs to me," he stated as he reached a hand out and pinched her nipple hard.

She moaned from the exquisite pain shooting through her.

He twisted her nipple and licked his lips with excitement at her response. "This belongs to me," he stated harshly as he reached down and took hold of her clitoris with his forefinger and thumb.

She closed her eyes and took a deep breath at his fiery touch.

"Does it not?" He pinched her harder.

"It does!" she cried out, forcing herself to keep her hands up in the air, giving him freedom to do as he wished.

"Spread your legs," he commanded, unwavering in his grip on both her nipple and clit.

She hesitated a moment, then slid her feet across the chilled floor, so they were spread past her shoulders. Before she could take another breath, she felt his finger invade her, pushing hard into her.

"This also belongs to me—your pain and your pleasure." He instructed her as though she hadn't already known these statements to be facts. "Everything about you belongs to me. You get pleasure when I allow it. You feel pain when I allow it, and you are happy with this." His voice remained calm over her vocal reactions to the pressure he put on her sensitive parts.

As quickly as he grabbed onto her, he let go. She felt the blood rush back into her nipple, and she bit her lip to keep from crying out at the burning that replaced the pinching.

She kept her eyes closed while he moved around the room. A chair scraped against the cement floor. The chains on the wall jangled.

"Come here," he directed.

She turned. Keeping her arms over her head, she walked to him with a graceful sway to her hips as he waited beside the chair, the one he used when he spanked her. Her stomach tightened.

"Sit," he commanded. "No, sit with your chest against the back of the chair." He corrected her.

She moved quickly to straddle the seat.

"Arms down."

She moved her feet to rest against the legs of the chair and put her arms around the back, folding them together. She awaited the ropes that would bind her in place.

"Stay in that position until I return. Do not move," he commanded and was gone.

She looked at the wall with confusion. Where had

he gone? What was he doing? She could move if she wanted. She could stand and stretch if needed.

She had betrayed him that morning when she'd slipped her vibrator out of the drawer of the nightstand. She had betrayed his trust and his authority when she smoothly inserted it into herself, deriving pleasure from the even vibrations and the light pinches she gave her erect nipples. The cries of pleasure that filled their bedroom when she found her release had sealed her fate.

Perhaps she'd wanted to be caught, to be punished for what she had done. She'd known she'd acted against the rules and against his wishes. She'd taken privileges where there were none to be taken. Maybe she had left the vibrator on the nightstand on purpose as she ran to the washroom to cleanse herself.

Now the door opened, and she could feel his presence. She was chilled; the draft from the door made her press into the chair, searching for some warmth. She did not turn her head to see him, but she could sense him near.

New tears burned her eyes. The thought of him playing over in his mind what she had done brought a new wave of shame.

He stood before his property, his most treasured possession, bringing her gaze to meet his with a tilt of her chin. He looked into her eyes and saw true remorse.

"You still wish to be mine," he stated. There was no question in his tone; he knew it as well as she. "You wish to be under my power, my control." He looked at her lips and wished he could kiss them, to take away her fear and remorse.

He remained strong as he knelt before her, reaching between the spindles of the chair. He traced her mound with a gentle touch of his fingertips, feeling the wetness a little lower.

"How did you come?" He looked at her as he

continued to fondle her. "Were you laying on your back?" he questioned further when he saw the confusion in her eyes.

"Yes." She nodded, her shaky voice barely audible.

"Did you use the vibrator to fuck yourself, or play with your clit?" He continued his pleasure torture.

"I…fucked myself with the vibrator and used my fingers on my clit." She closed her eyes. It embarrassed her to talk in such a way.

He openly smiled at her blush. He had done wicked things to her, fucked her in nearly every way imaginable, and yet she blushed when telling of her masturbation.

"I bought something a while ago, sure I would never have to use it, but it would appear I was wrong." He stood, leaving her tingling from his touch. "Stand up." He walked to the closet and disappeared for a moment, confident she would comply.

When he returned, he held the garment up to her eyes. In one hand, he held a black cotton thong. There was a small box sewn into the crotch. In his other hand, he held a leather thong. Two leather straps, one for her waist and one to cover herself from view or touch. The straps were held together with a lock.

Ignoring her pleading eyes, he crouched down and held out the black thong for her to step into. She instantly obeyed his order.

He slid the thong up into position and looked down at her. "I've always liked black on you."

His devilish smile comforted her, and she managed to smile meekly in return, as he worked to unbuckle the chastity belt.

She spread her legs for him without command, and he granted her an approving grin. He wrapped the leather strap around her waist and with exaggeratedly slow movements put the second strap through her legs, brushing against her sex as he did so.

He adjusted the belt so as not to make it too snug before locking it in place. Then he held the tiny key up to her nose. "I'll hold onto this." Smiling, he slipped the small, golden key into his pocket.

"There's a dress laying on the bed, go put it on." He stepped to the side, effectively dismissing her.

She left the basement in a rush to change, nearly tripping up the concrete stairs.

Standing in front of the bedroom mirror, she admired the panties and wondered how long she would have to endure the stiff leather between her legs.

The gentle vibrations of the thong startled her. She closed her eyes and focused on the pleasure the toy brought her as the pulsations intensified.

When they halted, she sighed with frustration. Hearing him calling for her, she quickly put on the dress he'd picked out for her—the blue dress, his favorite.

Before leaving the room, she looked at her nightstand. The keyhole was empty. She didn't need to test the drawer—he'd locked it.

She had truly disappointed him.

Her spirits lifted when a new wave of vibrations began their sweet dance, and she ran down the stairs to join him for supper.

Ever After

Her lover left a note of flowery endearments, his pledge of forever, and a promised ecstasy only they understood. His instructions had been simple, and she had followed them perfectly, obediently.

Her lover never returned home.

A freak accident, she was told. Her heart was broken and stopped beating shortly after.

Each All Hallow's Eve she can be heard in the tower room, readying herself for him, following his instructions.

"Strip nude, leave your hair down, do not leave the tower room… I will be home by dark."

The Simple Things

He took great pleasure in watching her undress for him on their bed. In particular, he loved to witness her panties make their way over her ankles and slip off her feet.

She seemed to slither out of her clothing, her feet never touching the ground.

Once her lacy panties had been carelessly tossed from the bed, she rolled onto her stomach and beckoned him with her grin. An invitation of sorts.

He stood beside the bed, admiring the smooth texture of her glowing ivory skin. He flashed a devilish smile as his fingers reached for the buckle of his belt.

She shivered.

Getting to the Bottom

The thing about putting something on the shelf to discuss at a later date, was that eventually that later date crashes into you. Not even expecting it, the date comes tumbling down like the overstuffed portion of your closet when trying to get a sandal down from the shelf.

I met Stephan six months ago through a college friend. He didn't turn out to be anything like I imagined he would be. Nothing like any previous man I dated and surely nothing like any guy I've ever met.

When he walked into the restaurant with Alec, the above mentioned friend, I tried to be smooth. Tried not to notice that he reminded me of Don Draper in almost every way—except his hair wasn't greased into place. It was neatly combed and seemed to stay where he put it simply by his command.

Authority filled his aura. Waitresses ran to him when he raised his hand for a fresh drink. Taxis pulled over for him, even on a Saturday night in the hustle and bustle of a Chicago evening. Even myself, the unruly middle child, found it too hard to disobey him when he gave a command.

Right away I obeyed him, mostly without even noticing he was giving directions. It just seemed the natural way of things. He said to sit at the end of the table, I sat there. He said to clear the table after dinner, I did.

His orders never came as orders. There was no barking, no yelling, no stomping of his foot. He stated what he wanted done, and it was done. I didn't mind it; hell, I barely even noticed it at first.

Sex was a bit more obvious. He was in charge, and there was no disputing that fact. His casual brown eyes melted into pools of chocolate when he felt lusty.

He directed traffic, giving me turn-by-turn instructions. "Take off your pants." His dictate would come while we snuggled on the couch.

"No, leave on your panties. Good, lay over my lap." He'd move to the center of the couch.

Sometimes this would result in a spanking—playful swats to get my juices flowing and his dick hard. Other times it was another way of snuggling. His large hands rubbing my ass while watching television.

At the beginning of our relationship, it became obvious there was something different about him. Not just the overflow of confidence he had, but the control he held over me. He explained about his previous relationships, that he was always in control of them. The Dominant. I was to be the submissive if we were to continue. A list of activities was given to me, and I was sent home to mull it all over.

Anal seemed to be the only activity we disagreed on. I said no and he said yes.

After a long discussion about it, he said, "Okay, we'll put that on the shelf for later. When we've been together longer, and you can trust me enough. The training is nearly as fun as the act," he finally decreed with a devilish look in his eye that reminded me of a young boy hiding a secret.

That shelf was not as high off the ground as I had hoped.

The small table in the kitchen of his condo stood next to the window—my favorite spot on Saturday mornings with its view of the city. I could see the lake if I stuck my head out and turned just a bit.

My half-eaten bagel lingered in my hand as I let my mind wander off to the afternoon he'd planned for us. A trip to the Art Institute. Like most guys I knew, Stephan wasn't a huge art lover, but he'd consented to an afternoon at the museum.

A low thud broke my trance, and I looked down at the tabletop where a small plug sat on my plate, next to my cup of coffee. I gazed up to find him standing with his arms folded over his naked muscular chest. I was most obedient when he looked in such a way. His pj bottoms clung to his narrow hips, low enough the thin trail of hair that led to his crotch caught my attention.

"What's that?" I pointed to the object with my bagel.

"That is a butt plug." He leaned over to kiss my cheek then headed to the fridge.

"Yeah, I know that. What I mean is…what is it doing on the table?" I continued to stare at the plug, as if it were going to jump off the table and bite me at any given moment.

The fridge closed; his feet made no sound as he stepped back to me. He squatted down on his haunches, bringing himself to my eye level. He snatched up the plug in his right hand and held it by the base as if he were showing me a beautiful bouquet of flowers.

"I want you to wear this while we are out this afternoon." His eyes were serious and latched onto mine.

I took a bite of my bagel.

He took the bagel from my hand and put it on the plate. "I'm serious."

"I know you are." I swallowed. "We agreed not to talk about anal." I pointed out.

"No. I agreed to shelve it for a while. It's been a while." He shrugged. "Besides, this isn't anal. This is a butt plug." His lips screwed up into a playful grin.

"I don't know." I took the plug from his hand. It felt

heavy and rubberlike.

"I want you to wear it while we're at the museum. You can take it out when we get to the restaurant for lunch. It'll be fun."

"Doubtful." I rolled my eyes.

He pinched my thigh.

"Sorry." Eye rolling was on the short list of thing I was not allowed to do in his presence.

"Shower up and meet me in the bedroom." He took my bagel from my plate and walked out of the kitchen, leaving me and the plug alone.

It was the longest shower of my life. Stephan came in to check on me three times, finally giving me a two-minute warning before he would drag me out rinsed off or not. I knew him well enough to believe him. He never gave a warning that he didn't follow through on.

I found him in the bedroom all dressed and ready to go, sporting a pair of well-worn jeans and a cover band T-shirt. In one hand he held the plug and the other held a small tube. His manner was casual, as though he were going to help me put on my shoes. I tried to ignore the presence of the plug as I applied my makeup and threw my hair into a decent do.

He tsked his tongue at me when I reached for my panties.

"Come here." He sat on the bed.

I took a deep breath.

"Now."

I padded over to the bed and held the towel in place around my chest.

"Drop the towel." He tried to mask his annoyance, but I could hear it building in his tone.

The towel pooled on the floor. "What if I say no to this? That I really don't want it," I asked him with my hands on my hips. I pushed the knowledge that I was naked and he was not from my mind.

He placed the items on the bed and took my hands in his. "Nothing happens here without your okay. If you really don't want to try this, then we won't. I think you're going to like it. I think you will find doing this for me will not only physically turn you on but will consume you mentally." He kissed my knuckles. "But you have to be okay with it." His willingness to let the subject drop while at the same time pushing me to try something new and push my boundaries played around in my mind.

"Okay. If I hate it, we can stop?" I asked.

"Just say your safeword, and it ends," he promised with excitement brewing in his eyes.

"Okay." I breathed out my consent.

"That's my girl." He yanked on my hands, pulling me down over the side of the bed and delivered three hard swats to my backside. The dampness along with the harshness of the swats made me cry out. "You know better than to put those fists on your hips like some fishwife."

"Yes. I'm sorry." I looked over my shoulder, hoping to find him smiling.

His lips were tight and his hand rested on my ass.

"Really. I'm sorry," I repeated myself. Sometimes I forgot how particular he could be about my stance when I talked to him.

His hand crashed down on me a few more times but with less urgency and more tenderness. He paused between each swat to knead my muscles. I turned into a gooey mess.

Just as I fell onto a soft mental cloud, I felt a cold gel being applied between my cheeks. He spread them wide and continued to rub lube over my tight asshole.

My face flushed with fire at the idea of him looking at such an intimate part. I didn't peek over my shoulder at him; instead, I clenched my eyes shut as he continued to work his finger into my hole.

"Relax, baby," he whispered, moving his finger further past the rim. "Relax. Take a deep breath and just relax." He moved his free hand further down to find my clit. His fingers knew me well.

"You are wet already, and I've barely begun with you." He sounded amused. "My good little slut."

My mind swirled with his trash talk. I was his slut, his good girl slut, who allowed him to play with her asshole.

His finger probed further still, the initial burning of his entrance subsided and the tingling feeling and craving for more began to take hold. I arched my back and pushed toward him, drawing more of him into me.

"Hungry slut." He chastised playfully. "Take it slow." He pulled out of me and began to inch his way back in.

Once he was able to get his full finger into my ass, he said, "Okay, now fuck it."

I pulled forward and moved back, the fullness and new sensations drove me to move faster. His fingers playing with my clit brought me to the very brink of fulfillment.

"Not yet." He yanked his finger away, leaving me feeling empty.

I looked over my shoulder at him, my mouth fixed in a pout. I heard the cap of the tube and felt the plug pressing against me next.

He didn't push it into me; instead, he continued to play rough with my clit and told me to take it in.

I pushed back against it, and it slid into place. The fullness was greater than his finger and the sensations around the puckering rim more intense. He held the base and told me to continue fucking his fingers. I moved and moaned as the fire in my belly built to white hot.

"Okay, go ahead." Permission granted.

I yelled out with the waves as they took me away from his bedroom.

I eventually floated back to him, draped over his bed, with a plug up my ass.

He tapped it a few times and let go of me. "That's my good girl." He kissed my left cheek and stood from the bed. "Get dressed, let's get this museum over with."

He handed me my clothes and left me to it.

Two evenings later I received a text from him just as I went to bed.

"Plug in" was all it said.

I dropped the phone onto my nightstand with a sigh. Having him insert the plug for me while bringing me to orgasm was one thing, having to put it in place myself was another. I pulled the plug out of my nightstand and grabbed the lube he gave me to keep at my apartment. I pulled my panties down to my knees and knelt on the bed on all fours.

My fingers danced over my clit.

The cell chirped again. "Don't touch yourself, just put it in."

I swore at the phone. The man was beginning to know me too well for my own good. I squirted the lube onto the plug and rubbed more around the rim of my asshole.

After some adjustments to my position, I was able to push it securely inside. I rested a moment with my head on the pillow to allow the burning to turn to sensual fullness before I pulled up my panties and slipped under the covers.

"It's in," I texted back and turned off my light.

"Good Girl." Those words displayed in a simple font on the screen of my phone sent shivers through me, as though his fingers were on my heart, stroking it.

I fell asleep easily that night.

"I have something for you," he whispered into my ear as I burrowed into his chest. He clicked the remote, ending our television for the evening. Neither of us were much of a couch potato, but it gave us an excuse to snuggle.

"If it's anything less than a big bowl of ice cream, I'm not sure I'm up for it." I placed a hand on his upper thigh, near the small bulge in his pants.

He pinched my ass and shoved me off him with his shoulder.

"No ice cream for you." He held out his hand to me.

I gave a fake pout and took it.

The bed was made in military fashion, the same as every other day. His amount of discipline for cleanliness truly was next to godliness, which is why most of our time was not spent at my apartment.

"Sit." He left me on the bed and went to the foot locker at the end of his bed. His toy chest. He rummaged around until he found what he was looking for.

"Kneel." He gave that command with his head still in the locker.

While he took his toy to the bathroom, I slid to the floor. My knees spread shoulder width apart, my hands turned palms up on my knees. I sat back on my heels and waited for him.

He returned with a big grin on his face, like he had just opened up the best Christmas gift he could ask for. He sat on the bed in front of me holding a new butt plug. This one was the largest to date and was in the shape of a ball.

My eyes widened.

"You've been using the larger plug this week, right?" he asked, looking into my eyes.

I nodded.

"Answer with your words." He tapped my lips with

his forefinger.

"Yes."

"I'm sorry?" He turned his head as though to get a better angle at my voice.

"Yes, Sir," I corrected myself.

"Good Girl." The dimple on his chin appeared. His eyes sparkled. "I think you are ready to take me in your ass." He balanced the plug on the palm of his hand. "But I want you to wear this for a bit first. Do you think you are ready?" He kept his eyes on me, searching me for my worries and my fears.

I eyed the black ball-shaped plug on his hand with concern. It was the largest of the plugs he'd introduced, and the closest to the width of his dick. "Okay. I think so," I whispered.

Anal sex had been on the shelf for a while, and during the time he'd waited for my consent, he had shown me patience, love, and tenderness. Every ache I held, he soothed, every itch I complained of, he scratched. Convinced that I would not find much pleasure in the actual act, I knew pleasing him in this way would bring me joy like none other.

Cautious eyes swept over my expression before he gripped the plug at the base and pointed it at my lips. "Open." He pressed the silicone ball to my lips.

After a quick swallow, I parted my lips enough for him to slip the plug past them.

"Close." He tapped my nose with his forefinger, an act that felt silly each time he did it, but he insisted on continuing.

"Now hold that in place. Hands up." He reached down and picked my shirt up from the hem and slid it easily over my breasts, then my arms.

"Remove your bra." He tapped my nose again, and I made quick work of unhooking the black satin bra and slid the straps down my arms, letting each breast bounce free from their restraining cups.

"I will never get used to your tits." He shook his head.

The first time he'd touched my breasts he'd told me they were beautiful. He held them in his palms and ran his thumbs over my nipples as he complimented them. He kissed them as he would a new pet, with care and love. He massaged them, remarking on how they overflowed his hands. When he was done loving them, he beat them with his riding crop. My hands were bound behind me as the stinging strokes reigned down on them.

I loved it.

It was with the same care that he helped me stand from my knees. He unbuttoned my jeans and pulled them down over my hips. My panties followed, and I was left standing naked, holding the black plug in my mouth.

He bent me over the bed and took out the lube from his nightstand. "Just like all of the other times." He ran his finger, with the cool gel on the tip, between my cheeks.

I buried my head between my hands.

He reached around me and pulled the plug from my mouth with a loud popping sound. I clenched my fists but tried to keep my ass from tightening. He spoke soothing words and used his hands to rub my cunt, which betrayed me every time we played this game by becoming wet without my consent. Knowing my body enjoyed his touches and his strokes, I focused on getting my mind to connect to the physical sensations.

"Relax." He spread my cheeks wide and tapped my asshole with his middle finger. I felt him slowly push past the rigid muscle, and he wiggled his finger. "That's better. You're getting much better at this. God, you're tight." His voice sounded strained.

His finger slid back out, and the plug replaced it. I

took a deep breath as he pushed the plug into place. The burning eased away quickly, leaving only the full feeling behind.

He tapped the base of the plug. "Good girl." He kissed the top of my ass, where the two cheeks met above the foreign object.

He helped me to stand and walked me to the mirror on his closet door. He spun me around so I was leaning into him, and my ass faced the mirror.

"Turn your head so you can see," he directed, and I obeyed.

The black base of the plug held my cheeks open where it sat in place. It appeared darker against my pale skin and larger than it had in his palm. He pulled me closer to him, sticking my ass out. He tapped the plug again, sending a jolt through my ass to my clit.

"Tell me what you see." His words sank into me.

I hated this part, this unveiling of my emotions and desires.

"I see a plug in my ass." I went with the obvious.

He slapped my ass hard. The movement of my cheek pushed against the plug. I grunted.

"I see the base of the plug. It's spreading my ass cheeks."

"And what is the plug doing on the inside." He ran his hand over my hair. He didn't look at me while he spoke, but I felt him watching us in the mirror.

"It's stretching me." I let out a deep breath with my answer.

"Give me more." He rubbed my arms.

"It's making me feel full." I leaned into his chest.

"That's good." He kissed my head. His fingers found my wet, swollen clit and stroked it in a lazy fashion.

"Go on." He prodded me with his words.

"I feel—" His fingers entered me, giving me

another jolt of excitement. "I feel used."

"Good or bad?" He stilled in his movements.

"Good." I turned my face from him.

He pulled me back to him, hiding was never allowed.

"Your cunt is soaking wet," he whispered into my ear, as he tucked my hair back to take my earlobe between his teeth. "You are hot and ready for me."

My juices rolled down my thighs. I could smell me on his fingers when he brought them to my face to turn my chin.

"I'm going to fuck you in the ass tonight." He looked me in my eyes. No joking, no twinkle. All business. "Go to the bed and kneel on all fours for me." He moved away from me to let me by.

I crept onto the bed and found a comfortable position. I held the pillows in my hands, ready to use them in case I needed to scream when he pushed into me. I did not want to disappoint him.

I heard his clothing being removed and a drawer open. More lube.

He positioned himself behind me, his fingers on my clit again, then in my cunt. "Fuck my fingers." He held his hand still as I pushed back against him. He inserted a third finger.

My clit brushed against his knuckles, and I pushed faster against him, hoping for more tension on my cunt. During this time, I didn't realize he had pulled the plug out of my ass and was slowly positioning his dick.

His head touched my rim, and instantly, I tightened up and held fast to the pillows. He slapped my ass.

"Relax. Keep fucking my fingers."

I began to move again; each thrust back brought the head of his dick to the brim of my asshole. Soon he began to put more pressure on my ass, and the tingling sensations turned into yearning. I wanted his dick in me.

I wanted to take him all into my ass. I pushed back harder.

"Does my little hungry slut want something?" I could hear his smile in his voice. "Tell me what you want."

I dropped my head into the pillows. I wanted him in me. I wanted his thick dick inside my asshole, filling me and pushing me. I wanted his fingers to dance over my cunt, bringing me to the fiery edge of orgasm.

He wanted me to say these things out loud.

"Do you want my cock in you?" he asked, taking pity on me.

"Yes, Sir." I nodded and pushed back toward him.

"Tell me correctly." He rubbed the head of his cock over my tight hole.

"I want your cock in my ass. Please." The last word escaped me in more a whine than a plea.

He pushed harder into me. His head entered me. The burning started again, and I froze. He grabbed my clit between his forefinger and thumb and rolled it around making me moan in pleasure and push against him—taking more of him in.

"So fucking tight," he ground out as he pushed against me until the length of him was all the way in me.

We froze in position. He rubbed my ass with his hands, massaging me and letting me adjust to the fullness.

"Breathe, baby, Breathe." He spoke softly, his fingers teetering over my skin. "When you're ready. You lead this for now." His words soothed me.

The tension in the rim of my hole subsided, leaving behind a warm tingling. I drew apart from him, allowing his shaft to work its way nearly out. Then I began to sink toward him again—taking him back inside.

The tingling increased; I wanted more.

I moved forward again, pushing back toward him

with more intensity. His hands were on my hips, his fingers dug into me.

"That's it. Work your ass. There you go." His voice was strained.

The more I moved, the easier it was to take his length back into me. The burning disappeared and left a yearning for him.

He began to move his hips with me as I rocked back and forth on his cock. "Reach under the pillow." He stilled his movements.

I slid my hand under his pillow, and my fingers found a small bullet vibrator. He thought of everything. I flipped the small switch on the side of the miniscule pink bullet and placed it above my clit, groaning with the pleasure of it.

The vibrations teased my clit while his hard dick continued to shoot erotic waves through my asshole. I leaned my forehead on the pillow as I began to meet his thrusts with more fever. The initial discomfort melted into a heat that radiated through my body, starting at the small, once untouchable, hole.

"I want to see you." He pulled out of me, leaving an empty feeling behind.

I glared at him over my shoulder.

He responded with a sharp slap to my thigh. "Over on your back." He helped me turn around and knelt between my open thighs.

His large, calloused hands gently held my thighs apart and pushed back on them until his destination came into view.

"Will this work?" I swallowed hard.

He grunted a laugh.

"Oh, yeah. This will work. Put the vibrator back on your clit. There you go." His eyes fixated on me as I began to work the bullet over my clit then lower.

A rush fell over me with his watchful stare. His

arousal escalated with each moan and slight arch of my hips. His tongue slid over his bottom lip, and his eyes rolled back as he growled his frustration.

"Do you like when I play with my cunt for you?" I heard myself asking. Words normally kept in books and pornography movies rarely passed my lips, but with his erotic stare and his beautiful cock pointed at me, the words seemed to spill more freely.

"Baby, I love damn near everything you do." He grinned at me, putting himself into primal position. "Hold your legs up like this. I want to get back in that ass. Don't lose me, keep your eyes on me. Understand?" He pinched the inside of my thigh.

I winced. "Yes." A sharper pinch. "Sir! Yes, Sir!" I rectified my error and placed the bullet back on my clit as his dick descended to my dark utopia. I bit my lip hard as he began to enter me. It was smoother this time, no discomfort. The angle of being on my back pushed him toward my cunt, making the fullness even more enjoyable. I pressed harder on my clit and tried to arch up at him.

He held my hips down and shook his head.

Words appeared to be beyond him as he tried to control the pace of his thrusts. He wanted to pound into me; I could see the strain in his arms as he moved within me.

"Oh, yeah." He groaned. "This is much better. Play with your clit, harder." His jaw clenched, his biceps bulged with restraint.

My own ecstasy seemed within reach. My clit swelled beneath the attention the bullet paid it; my ass tingled with his thrusts. His fingers dug into my hips as he pushed deeper into me.

"I need to…" I moaned. "Please. I need to…" I clenched my eyes, trying to stave off the inevitable orgasm that was to crash down on me.

"Tell me what you need." His tone was soft, controlled.

"I need to come. Please. I need to come." I opened my eyes and stared into his.

He smiled, a slow, lazy smile that I would have thought him incapable of at such a time.

"Come for me." He slowed his thrusts and focused his attention on my expression.

I pressed the bullet harder into my clit, letting the vibrations drive me over the edge of a canyon that sent me into a free fall of waves of pleasure I'd never experienced before.

As I felt myself land and my mind refocus on the reality of where I was, he began to move quicker in me. His face relaxed, his fingers loosened their grip on my hips as he moved with more heat than before. He dove deeper into me; I touched his chest with my fingertips. A low growl escaped his clenched lips. An idea came over me.

I slid the bullet beneath me, to rest near my ass. I turned the power higher and instantly felt vibrations ripple through the brim of my ass. I spied a glance at his expression. His eyes widened and his mouth opened in shocked silence. I grinned.

He thrust harder and faster, and I held my ground, taking the pounding he needed to dish out. His fingers dug into my skin, and he thrust quickly, deeply into me, and I felt his dick begin to convulse inside me. The hot liquid of his cum filled me.

He took a deep cleansing breath, and I removed the bullet.

His disheveled hair gave him a boyish appearance, but the tension in the muscles of his chest and arms reminded me of the strong man I'd fallen in love with.

He slipped out of me and slid across the bed until he laid beside me, wrapping me in his arms. He kissed my temple.

"You okay?" His concern for me always peeked through first.

"Yeah. I'm good." I nodded.

"You took a good pounding." He rubbed my ass cheeks.

"You gave a good pounding," I countered. "I'm fine, really. Just a little…er…stretched." I giggled at my own phrasing; he tightened his arms around me.

"Let's take a shower and get all this lube off of us. You can wash the bedding while I make us a treat." He seemed reluctant to leave the comfort of the bed and pulled me along to the bathroom.

After washing and dressing in a cotton weave skirt and T-shirt, I stripped the bed, rolling the dirty sheets into a ball. The scent of the lavender dryer sheets still lingered on the clean bedding I placed over the bed. He disliked lavender but bought them because it was my favorite scent. I disliked wearing skirts, but wore them because he loved them on me.

I grabbed the detergent from the hall closet and walked through the kitchen with the basket of dirty sheets.

"I'm gonna take these down to the laundry room." I kissed his bare shoulder as he worked over the stove. Even with all the fancy cookware he had in his kitchen, he still made popcorn over the stovetop.

"Okay." He shook the pot as kernels began to dance within. "I put a cushion on the floor in the living room. When you get back, I want you to sit there while we watch our movie." He continued to shake the pot.

"At your feet?" I paused in the doorway. He'd never asked me to do that before.

"Yes." He didn't look at me. He didn't need to, no explanation was needed. He wanted me to sit on a cushion at his feet—on the extremely large, plush cushion that turned out to be much more comfortable than the couch.

I left him shaking the popcorn pot in his pajama bottoms and went to wash all of the sex out of the sheets. His sheets. Then I would sit at his feet on my cushion. His girl on her cushion at his feet.

My heart felt heavy with affection. It was another step forward. A step he took with me.

Always with me.

The Grass is Always Greener

Fresh cut grass is one of those scents that transports me somewhere else, to another time. A time where innocence was expected and a longing for the future to claim me mingled together.

I spent my youth helping my parents run their landscaping business. Some clients thought it odd for a teenage girl to be running the lawnmowers over their large plots of land or using the automatic sheers to prune their forgotten bushes, but only a few ever commented on it.

"That girl has a great head on her shoulders! She'll be running this business in a few years." My father would puff out his chest and boast to his friends. He wasn't wrong.

Two years after my high school graduation he passed away, a sudden heart attack while shoveling snow. He was forty-nine.

My mother ran the books while I supervised the work crews. We had to hire a small group of workers since the company had grown large enough I couldn't handle the load of clients on my own. College was pushed to the back burner. Mom needed me.

Mom didn't take Dad's passing lightly. She changed her eating habits, throwing away all junk food and soda from the house. Each morning at five o'clock, she'd wake up and head out for a three-mile walk. It didn't take long for her to drag me out of bed to keep her company. A quick shower and breakfast then we'd head out to work.

Jason Stonewall owned the only other landscaping business in our small town. Competition didn't rule either of our companies. There was enough work for us both to prosper. In fact, several times over the years we'd each needed to ask the other to take a client at one point or another because we were full.

Jason hadn't always owned the company on his own; it was a family business like ours. The reins were passed to him after his father's retirement a year ago. The difference was his company was getting even larger than ours, taking on clients outside of Christian County. A rumor was milling around town that Jason was biding his time before making an offer to buy us out.

Mom shooed the rumor away like an annoying gnat buzzing around her head. She'd never sell.

During a pit stop at Starbucks, I ran into Jason. Our paths hadn't crossed for nearly two years; most of our dealings were by telephone or through our fathers. If he hadn't smiled his notorious smile, I would have walked right past him.

Once I noticed him, it was hard to ignore his presence. It was obvious he'd been working with a crew that morning, evidenced by the dirt and fertilizer on his jeans. His shirt, clean, clung to him, enhancing his biceps and showcasing his sculpted chest. Deep green eyes swept over me with his greeting, a lopsided grin let a dimple loose on his cheek, and his tousled mild chocolate hair gave him a carefree look.

I wondered momentarily why I had never noticed his hotness before that moment. I decided it had been too long since my last date.

He bought my coffee. I declined the offer, and he declined to listen. He walked me to a table.

I mentioned I needed to get back to the crew; he pulled out the chair and told me to sit. I sat. Something in the way he carried himself and the tone he used reeked of authority. He didn't carry arrogance in his voice. It was confidence.

The conversation started with small talk, catching up with each other's lives and family news. Jason graduated four years ahead of me, so we'd never known each other during school. Landscaping was our only tie.

His casual glance at the collar of my V-neck white cotton T-shirt brought a blush to my cheeks as I tried to nonchalantly adjust it, so my cleavage would be less noticeable. With a D cup, that wasn't an easy task.

"So, I hear you are going to be making my mom an offer on the company," I blurted out during a moment of silence. His eyes wandered over my expression.

"Really?" He raised an eyebrow, and his lips thinned out.

I wondered if I crossed a line.

"Do you think your mom would sell?" A slow question.

"No. She won't." I straightened my shoulders. If buying my coffee was a prelude to trying to buy my mom out, I wanted to get that out on the table.

"Okay. Then I guess there's no point in asking her." He shrugged and sipped his coffee. "Do you want her to sell?" he asked with a tilt of his head.

I played with the cardboard ring around my cup. "No. Of course not." I scoffed. It was fake and he knew it.

"Did you ever go to college? If I remember, my dad used to tell me about some music program you were in. You played the piano or something?" He narrowed his eyes, searching his memory.

"Yeah. I played the piano. Your dad sponsored the little music club down at the youth center." I nodded, amazed he would remember such a small part of my history from so long ago.

"Do you still play?"

"No." I shook my head and fidgeted in my seat. A dream long ago forgotten, and I wanted it to stay that way.

"My dad loved music. I remember him bragging about you constantly after he'd peek in on the lessons at the center." He smiled with the memory. "I remember, because it made me hate you for making him so proud. All I ever could do was throw a football or swing a bat."

"Your dad was proud of you." I moved to the defense.

"Oh, I know. We were kids then." He grinned. "He'd be a bit disappointed you gave it up. Why'd you give it up?" He pushed.

My eyes wandered out the window over his shoulder to my truck, the beat up Chevy with the original logo of the company on the door. A mower sat in the bed.

Jason followed my gaze and nodded knowingly. "The family business."

"It's fine. After Dad died, Mom needed me. Keeping the business going is more important. College will wait." I kept my eyes from him as I lied.

We sat in silence again. His eyes narrowed as he inspected my expression.

"When's the last time you did something just for you?" He leaned forward across the table. The smell of his mocha floated between us. His hand rested on mine.

An electric current shot up my arm; my breath caught in my throat for a moment. Too long since a man touched me.

"I really need to get back." I pulled my hand away from his touch.

He reached out and grabbed my elbow, keeping me in my chair. I swallowed. His eyes met mine. Determination hid beneath the cool color of his eyes.

"When's the last time you were kissed?" He leaned forward and brushed his lips against mine.

My eyes fluttered closed as he came back toward me; his lips pressed against mine, capturing me. He ran his tongue along my lower lip until I parted my lips to allow him entrance as he deepened the kiss.

I dropped my keys on the table, a fire sparking within me. I felt my thighs shake; my panties moistened at his touch.

When he pulled back from me, I was left in a daze. I opened my eyes sure I'd find a cocky grin on his face. His soft smile surprised me.

"Are your panties wet?" His question shocked me. "Don't answer. I'm sure they are." His voice became husky.

I tried to form words. I failed.

"Tonight, I want you to come to my condo. Arrive at exactly seven o'clock. Wear a sundress, a light colored one. No panties and no bra. You won't need them."

He kissed my cheek, dropped a piece of paper in front of me, and stood from the table. "Seven." He patted my shoulder and left me.

"What?" Finally a word came to me. He was gone. I sat for a few minutes until I was sure he'd left and headed back to the crew.

Jason was nuts.

The kiss stayed on my mind all throughout the afternoon. Several times I found myself staring off into the sunlight lost in the memory of his lips. Living in a small town left a girl with few choices of men. Being a landscaper by trade wasn't a big turn on to most of the men in town. They wanted ladies who would give them big strapping boys who would grow up to be football players. I couldn't remember any of the half dozen kisses I'd received from a man to have a lasting effect as Jason's did.

Mom's meatloaf sat on the stove when I got home. She stood at the counter mashing potatoes. "I used ground turkey for the meatloaf; it'll taste the same," she promised.

"Uh. I might go out tonight." I leaned against the counter. "Yeah. I think I might." I left her staring after me with an open mouth while I left to hit the shower.

In the car, I pulled out the small paper Jason gave me with his address on it. A short drive later, I found myself parked in front of his condo building. Five minutes until seven.

I took a deep breath, reminded myself I could leave if I became uncomfortable, and shoved myself in the direction of the front lobby.

He opened the door with little flare. His eyes drank me in from my face to my toes. He smiled with approval of my light yellow sundress and stepped out of the way to let me in. "You're early." He took my purse and put in on the hall table.

I looked at my watch.

"I said exactly seven." He kissed my cheek. "It's okay. You'll learn." He kissed me again, this time on my lips.

I put my hands on his shoulders to steady myself. A sharp slap to my ass startled me, and I pulled away.

"I'm strict, but extremely rewarding." His voice was casual.

I covered my backside with my hands. He walked away from me. I stood still.

He came back into the hall when he realized I wasn't with him. "Did you hate that?" he asked, no concern evident in his tone.

I shook my head.

"Then come here." He held out his hand for me.

I walked to him, unsure of what I had gotten myself into.

"Stand here." He placed me in the center of the room. The coffee table and couch both had been shoved toward the wall, leaving an empty space. "You give up everything to help your mom. You gave up so much of your free time in high school to help your parents with the business. What has it gotten you?" He circled me as he spoke.

"Well—"

"Do you enjoy mowing grass and pulling weeds?" he asked with a harsh tone.

"Well, it's not—"

"Yes or no." He stopped walking and stood behind me.

I wanted to turn to him, to see him, but something in his tone told me not to.

"No." My shoulders sagged with the relief of that truth. I felt his hands on my hair.

He gathered it into one hand, twisting it around his fist. This gave him complete control of my head. He pulled it to the left, leaving my neck open to his lips. He nibbled below my earlobe, then lower to my shoulder.

"Such a good girl," he whispered over my skin. "Take off your dress," he commanded and let my hair fall over my back.

I paused only a moment before I complied. Moisture gathered on my thighs. The sound of his voice alone made my pussy wet.

I dropped the dress on a nearby chair. He continued to circle me, inspecting me. He stopped in front of me and gathered my breasts in his hands. He didn't look at them; he kept his eyes on mine. I tried to look over his shoulder, away from his deep stare.

"I want your eyes. Don't look away from me. Ever," he commanded. His tone was firm, unyielding.

I brought my gaze back to him.

He smiled. "You have beautiful tits." His compliment came with a squeeze of my breasts, as though he was picking a ripe fruit at market. "How do I not remember these tits?"

I swallowed. His words made me uncomfortable. Having been the tomboy type most of my life, I hadn't had anyone look twice at my body, much less speak openly to me about it. His thumbs ran over my erect nipples, and he leaned in for a kiss.

His lips were soft against mine, testing the waters at first with little pecks. Each one made me hungry for the next. Finally, he seized my lips beneath his. His tongue urged my lips to part for him, and he claimed my mouth. His teeth bit at my lips; his tongue swept through me. He tasted of honey.

I put my hands on his hips, to hold myself up as much as to feel his strength.

His work jeans had been replaced by casual dark slacks, his T-shirt abandoned for the button down white collar shirt he wore. He looked more the executive than the landscaper. He looked powerful and his waist felt narrow beneath my hands, but I could feel the muscles of his stomach.

He dragged his lips away from me, placing a chaste kiss to the tip of my nose. "Tonight is about you." He stepped further away from me and crossed his arms over his broad chest. "You give to everyone without taking for yourself. You enjoy giving to others, and that is the part of you that I want to capture—but first, you must learn to let yourself free of their expectations. You need to know it's okay to have pleasure and want pleasure. You get satisfaction out of helping your parents with the business. You'll get the same satisfaction following my rules and serving me. However, I don't simply take and take. I give back."

I tried to follow his words, but my mind stuck on the word "rules".

With my hands folded in front of me, I became very aware of my nakedness and tried to cover up.

He shook his head. "Never hide from me. That means your body and your mind. Your gaze is always to be on me. Hands behind your back, fold your arms just above your ass. I want full access," he explained.

I didn't move.

"Stephanie, do as I tell you. I don't like repeating myself." He used my full name. Everyone called me Stephie.

I remained frozen—unsure of what to do.

He moved to me quickly with a heavy sigh. He pulled my arms behind me and put them in the position he wanted. "Like this."

I gripped the elbows of my opposite arms.

He held my hands with one of his own and delivered three sharp slaps to my naked bottom with the other.

I jumped at the surprise and sting of them. "Wait." I finally found my tongue and tried to pull away, but he held on to me. "I don't know…why…" I floundered.

He rubbed away the sting with his palms. The electric current was back to running through my spine.

"Your ass bounces perfectly," he whispered into my ear.

My mind whirled.

"Now, slide your feet apart until they are lined up with your shoulders." His warm breath settled on my shoulder.

I inched my feet apart.

"Wonderful." He kissed my neck and wrapped his hands around me to fondle my breasts again.

I tilted my head to give him better access to my neck. My pussy clenched; my clit ached to be touched.

As if he knew my thoughts, he removed his hands from my breasts and trailed them down past my stomach, past the narrow nestle of curls until he reached my clit. "Wet." He kissed my ear as his finger rubbed my sensitive nub in circles.

A groan escaped my lips, and I leaned back into him. The sensations of his fingers on me ran up into my belly. I closed my eyes from the intensity of it.

"I knew you'd react this way." He pinched my clit, bringing me to attention again.

I wiggled in his embrace.

He chuckled in my ear before letting go of my clit.

"Tell me what this feels like," he instructed as he began toying with my swollen nub again. "Do you like my touch?"

"Yes," I whispered and arched my hips toward his hand, wanting more of it.

He pulled his hand away and placed a light slap to my pussy. I moaned but didn't try to avoid the second. A rush of adrenalin ran through my veins. I wanted more. I needed more.

"So damn good." He licked my shoulder and released me.

I felt cold with his body gone from me.

He walked to the couch and leaned against the arm of it. "If your dad hadn't passed away, would you have kept up with the piano?" His question threw me off guard.

The physical sensations he'd just caused still swirled through me; his abrupt change in momentum took a moment to adjust to.

"I don't know." My answer was honest. I tried not to think about what might have been. It would change nothing.

"One day I'll ask you to play something for me. Will you do it?" His face held a casual expression, as though we were back at the coffeehouse chatting about old times.

"I guess so." I shrugged. His conversation while I stood before him exposed unsettled me. I fidgeted in my stance, but did not change positions.

"When I ask you a yes or no question, the only response I want to hear is a yes or a no." His tone didn't change.

I wasn't being dressed down, only corrected. The act aroused me as though his fingers were back on me.

"When I ask you to play for me, will you?"

"Yes." I nodded.

His approval reached his green eyes. They melted when he was pleased with my answers. I felt an urgency to see that look more often.

"What will you play for me?" His question was lighthearted.

My frustration at wanting his hands back on me must have been showing in my expression. I searched my memory for a song I might remember.

"Lake Erie Rainfall." I recalled the song his father had enjoyed most when I'd played at the youth center.

His smile warmed. He remembered the song, too.

"Come to me." He remained where he sat.

I took one step toward him, then another—keeping my hands behind me. My elbows ached. Once I reached him, he took my breasts in his hands again. This time he remained silent as he kneaded them and pulled at my nipples. He looked at me and gave me a slow wink as he brought his tongue to my breast. I let out a loud breath and arched toward him.

Every touch felt electric hot. He wrapped his lips around my areola and used his tongue to toy with my nipple. Sliding his free hand down my body, he found my wetness again. He tapped my thighs, a signal to widen my stance.

Once I stood properly, he slid a finger between my slick lips and into my pussy. I groaned with hunger at the new feeling. His thumb brushed my clit as he pumped his fingers in and out of me. His mouth didn't leave my breast.

I tried to keep my eyes on him, but the sensations were too powerful. I closed my eyes and rolled my head back to focus on his touches. I knew I should be ashamed at having this man I barely knew touching me in such ways. I shouldn't be going along with him, but I didn't feel ashamed. I felt empowered. I felt sexy and wanted. I needed him.

"You are so fucking hot. So tight." He pulled away from me and grinned. "When's the last time you were properly fucked?" He slowed the rhythm of his fingers.

"Define properly." I found my own smile.

He laughed. "Okay, fucked then. When is the last time you had a cock in you?" His words sounded dirty, but each one placed another log onto an already white hot fire burning inside of me.

"A year ago," I whispered my answer, embarrassed.

He probably got laid weekly with his looks and confidence, and extremely well trained hands. He let out a low whistle.

"Was it good?" He kissed my stomach as he asked his question.

"No." I gave a correct answer.

He nuzzled my breast with his nose.

I heard him whisper I'm a good girl, and my cunt got even wetter. His fingers picked up speed and intensity. His eyes locked with mine again. My elbows ached, but I managed to ignore them and focus on what he was doing to my cunt.

"So fucking hot." He growled and pulled free of me.

I whimpered at the loss of his touch. He held my

elbows in his hands and carefully brought my arms back to my sides. A painful burning rushed through my joints at the new position.

He rubbed the discomfort away. "Do you want me to fuck you?" he asked still rubbing my arms. I wanted him to rub my cunt.

"Yes," I answered, sure of what I was saying. His question didn't involve one fuck; there was a deeper level.

"I don't fuck a woman just once and let her go." He backed up what I already knew. "I never fuck and run."

He stood from the couch. "I've noticed you around town for the past several months. Always so busy you never noticed me, or any of the other dozen men in town who stare at you when you walk by." He picked up my hand and walked me to his bedroom down the hall from the living room.

We stood next to the bed, his hands running over my bare arms. "You volunteer at the youth center," he said.

I wrinkled my brow at his knowledge.

"Sue's daughter is in your music group." His older sister had moved back into town a year ago with her two children.

I hadn't placed the little girl as being Sue's.

"You haven't really given up on the piano; you just give the kids a chance that you think is gone for yourself." He kissed my nose again. The playful affection still sent shivers through me.

"Why does this matter right now?" I finally asked.

"Because I want you to know I'm not into you just because you're hot. And you are extremely hot. It's everything. Your devotion and loyalty to your family. Your fierceness and your passion. It's all fucking hot. Your beautiful tits don't hurt either, but even without them, I'd want to bury my dick in you and own you."

I raised my eyebrows at his words.

"Own you," he repeated. "I don't share what's mine, and once I fuck you, you're mine." His voice held a tenderness that calmed my nerves. "Before you get in my bed, you have to know that. I don't fuck just for the hell of it."

I watched his expression. His confidence dominated his gaze, but there was a small piece of concern that drew me to him. His words were making him vulnerable to me. I could reject him, and he would be hurt. I had no intention of doing either.

"Okay." I nodded, bumping his chin with my head.

"Okay, what?" he asked, searching my eyes.

"Okay, Sir?" I tried, and he laughed.

"That word sounds beautiful on your lips, but what I meant was…are you agreeing to continue on or are you saying, okay, see you later?"

"Oh. The first thing." I smiled at him.

He took my face in his hands and kissed me. A hungry kiss, there was no gentleness to it. He crushed me with his lips, and I melted into it.

He didn't break away as he unbuttoned his shirt and pulled it free from his body. I explored the muscles on his chest with my hands as he unbuckled his belt. I heard his pants drop to the ground, and he moved to step out of them. He pulled away from me to remove his boxers, and I looked down at his cock.

Although it had been at least a year since seeing a man's dick, I knew a beautiful one when I saw it. Taking the initiative, I wrapped my fingers around the base of him. His growl urged me on.

I moved my hand toward the head, keeping pressure on his shaft as I did so. Another growl rose into the air. He felt swollen in my fingers; I could feel his urgency beneath my grasp.

"Next time, I want your pretty lips around my dick.

You on your knees looking up at me with my cock in your mouth. But that's next time." He pushed me onto the bed and joined me, kneeling between my legs. He ran his hands down my thighs, reaching my wet cunt. His fingers drove into me, and I arched upward at the feeling.

"Reach on the nightstand. In that small cup." His voice was hoarse.

I reached over and found the rubber he sought.

Keeping his eyes locked with mine, he slid the rubber down his shaft. Once that detail was taken care of, he placed the tip of his dick at the edge of my hungry pussy.

"Tell me again what you want." His stare darkened.

"I want you to fuck me." I smiled what I hoped was a seductive smile.

"See how accommodating I can be." His lips curled into his own evil grin, and he slowly slipped into me.

I could feel my pussy stretch to take his size. Every bit more of me he entered created a new sensation of being filled. I tried to push upward at him, but he held my hips down to the bed.

"I'm leading." He reminded me.

I bit my lower lip and tried to remain still as he filled me with his cock.

I felt his nestle of curly hair on my clit and knew he was fully embedded. I dug my fingernails into his shoulders. He pulled out at a torturously slow pace, and I moaned my frustration.

"Please," I begged as he began to push back into me.

"Tell me what you want."

I could see the restraint in his eyes wavering. My own left me long ago.

"Fuck me!" I bucked beneath him. He laughed.

"I am," he teased.

"No. Really fuck me. I can't take this slow shit. Please." I gripped him harder.

"I knew you'd please me," he whispered just above my lips before he captured them in another passionate kiss. He drove into me hard.

I groaned from the force of the pleasure it brought me. He pulled back and pushed into me again.

Hot lust ran the room now. I felt his balls slap against my ass with each of this thrusts, and I began to meet each of his pumps. He didn't stop me and kept to his rhythm. His hands roamed to my tits, and he growled into my ear as he continued to thrust into my willing cunt.

I pulled my legs up toward my chest, spreading them further. His fierce groan told me I'd done the right thing. I hooked my hands behind my knees and took his thrusts with satisfaction.

"Fuck, you're so hot. Touch your tits for me," he ordered in a strangled voice.

I began pinching my nipples and pushing my breasts together. His pleasure at the sight before him drove me closer to my undoing. He ran his tongue over his bottom lip, and I imagined it on my pussy.

He reached between our bodies and found my clit. His forefinger pressed down on it as he drove into me again and again. I could hear our bodies slamming together in the room, and I clenched my teeth. The fire in my belly was about to explode.

"Come for me. Come all over my cock." He put more pressure on my clit and pushed into me with more speed and force.

I needed no further encouragement; intense waves crashed into me knocking me out of reality. I rode the waves as they took over the room and gently brought me back to the bed where I lay beneath him. His eyes never left me as I found my orgasm.

I had only a moment to land safely back onto the pillow before his hands gripped my hips, and he pounded into me with a loud roar of pleasure.

I watched him as he rode his own waves of ecstasy, and I ran my fingers over his shoulders until he landed safely with me once more.

We laid in silence, our breaths racing together in time. He pulled me to him and snuggled with me as our chests began to slow, and we recovered our breath.

"That was even better than I'd pictured in my mind." He kissed my head.

"Stephanie, are you okay?" he asked after a few more moments of silence.

"Yes," I answered. My cheeks flushed with the images of what we had done.

"Embarrassed?" He kissed my earlobe from behind.

"No. Yes. I don't know." I wiggled from his grasp and turned to face him. "I don't know you very well," I admitted.

He nodded.

"I mean, you are the competition after all."

"Our parents never saw it that way." He pointed out.

"You do want to buy my mom out," I accused in a soft tone.

He nodded again. "Sure, having your client list would grow our company. But you said she'd never sell. So not an issue." He kissed my nose. "I didn't ask you over tonight for that." He sounded insulted.

"I know." I sighed. "You must have a ton of women falling at your feet. Why would you want me?" It was an honest question.

"You are real." His answer was given in a simple, matter of fact way. "If you don't stop moving your hips like that against my hand, I'm going to fuck you again. And I'm sure you're going to be pretty sore from that last round." A smile hinted in his eyes.

I blushed more. "May I get dressed?"

"Sure. After we clean up." He slid from the bed and pulled me along to his two-person wide bathtub.

We took our time bathing in the large tub. He washed my hair with a honey scented shampoo. The intimacy warmed me.

The evening ended with him walking me to my car. He wanted me to stay the night, but I explained my mother would worry. He opened the door for me, and once I had the car started, he leaned down to my window.

"Two months." He held up two fingers at me.

I wrinkled my brow in confusion.

"You have two months before I make you pack your stuff and move out of your mom's house."

"Don't you think it's a little forward to have me move in with you already?" I asked in a cheeky tone.

"With me or not with me, in two months you are to be out of your mom's house." His tone was back to firm.

I shook my head. "She needs me."

"No. She doesn't. Not like that." He placed his two fingers over my mouth when I began to protest again. "Two months." He leaned in the window and kissed me.

I sighed when he broke away.

"I'll call you tomorrow morning. I'd like to have lunch with you." He stepped away from the car, so I could pull out. "Sleep well." With that, he waved me on.

I drove away from his curb, watching him fade away in the rearview mirror.

That night, the warmth of his kiss lingered on my lips until I drifted off to sleep. A deep, satisfied sleep.

About The Author

Measha Stone lives in a quiet suburb outside Chicago with her husband and three kids. She has loved romance novels since being introduced to them in high school. Now as an adult, she has taken her love of romance and thrown in her love of all things kinky and erotic to create her own fantasy world.

To learn more visit her website at www.meashastone.com or blog at www.meashaswritings.blogspot.com
Follow her @Meahsa_Stone
Like her on facebook
www.facebook.com/authormeashastone

.

Hidden Heart

Chapter One
The Meet

True love was a myth spread among generations of single women to encourage them to continue their search for the man of their dreams. Jessica Stanley knew better. She'd called off the hopeless scavenger hunt a year after turning twenty-five.

Men weren't what the romance novels promised. Jake had educated her about the death of chivalry during their six months together their senior year at UIC. Harrison had explained with each lying breath how honesty and honor no longer made the modern man. Several others had taught her the same lessons over and over until she finally closed up shop and decided it was better to remain single.

This wasn't to say Jessica didn't love men. She did. They brought many physical attributes to a relationship; however, those could be replaced by quality batteries and well-crafted machinery.

No, she would stick to nights out with good friends and lonely weekends buried in books.

Friday nights were reserved for dinner out with old friends. A small group that banded together during college and still lived near the city. Alex was one of her closest friends, so she was able to forgive him for being a part of the male cult of society. He had nursed her through several break-ups, and never once did he mutter the words I told you so, even though—more than once— he had in fact told her so.

It was Alex's pick for dinner, and Jessica was thankful he chose the Italian restaurant down the street from her. She hated fighting for a cab on the weekends with all of the newly twenty-one crowd jumping from bar to bar. The walk to the restaurant provided a nice release from her day at the law firm. The grind of working as a paralegal for one of the partners had left her mentally drained. The crisp air of autumn calmed her and cleared away all of the stress of the previous week. She was ready for relaxation and fun.

Most of her group beat her to the restaurant. The hostess pointed her in their direction, the back corner of the bistro, hidden from most of the restaurant. Jessica wiggled between chairs and tripped over someone's coat before she managed to get to them.

"Jessica!" Erin, her old roommate at UIC, stood up and threw her arms around her. White Diamonds perfume enveloped her as much as Erin's arms did.

Jessica took a deep breath through her mouth and grinned.

"I wasn't sure you'd make it! Alex said you were working on some big case this week." Erin took her seat.

"It's nearly finished, and I'm not thinking about it tonight." Jessica shimmied out of her coat and took a seat beside Jonathan, Erin's fiancé.

"I hear Alex is bringing a new guy tonight." Kelly, Erin's perpetual third wheel, chimed in after a long sip of her appletini. Her tone suggested more than an offering of information.

"I think he mentioned something. I haven't really talked to him this week. Maybe you'll find your true love." Jessica rolled her eyes at Kelly, who seemed to perk up at the idea.

"You aren't still thinking to stay celibate the rest of your life, are you?" Jonathan asked as he tried waving down a waiter with his empty beer bottle.

"No. I'm just not wasting time on searching for the catch of my life." Jessica smoothed down her windblown chestnut hair.

"Look at us." Erin linked her arm through Jonathan's and smiled. "We're happy. It is possible to find a great guy who makes you happy."

Jessica rolled her eyes at the sappy sentiment, fully ignoring her own twinge of envy pulling at her heart. Jonathan continued his search for a waiter.

"Ooh, now that is a good looking man." Kelly straightened her shirt and rushed a finger comb through her thick red curls while keeping her eyes fixed on her prey.

Jessica followed Kelly's stare. Alex was pushing his way through the tables toward them, a man walking behind him. A tall man. A tall man with undeniably handsome features. A tall, hot man, wearing a suit and looking very much a like a character straight off the set of Mad Men. His hair was a dark shade of brown, too dark to be brown and too light to be black. Whatever the name of the color, it accentuated his azure eyes.

Jessica found herself holding her breath and had to remind herself to breath. He was just a guy.

"Sorry we're late. The damn cab got lost. I had to get him back here. Did you order appetizers yet? I'm starving!" Alex plowed through a small crowd of people and burst out at their table. He shrugged off his coat and threw it over the back of a chair. "Everyone, this is Royce. Royce, this is everyone. Jessica, Erin, Jonathan, and Kelly. I need to piss. Jess, get me a beer would ya?" Alex disappeared before anyone could react to the new member of their group.

"Whirlwind, that guy." Royce broke the awkward silence. Kelly laughed like a nervous high school girl. Jessica mentally vowed if Kelly started to bat her eyelashes she'd throw water at her.

"You can sit, you know." Jessica waved a hand at the empty seat beside Alex's coat. "He'll be back in a few minutes and will completely monopolize the evening."

Royce took his seat with a smile. Not an awkward smile but a controlled, casual grin. Kelly was close to drooling on her plate.

"Royce. That's an uncommon name." Kelly rested her chin on her fist with a wide smile from across the table.

"I'm afraid my mother may have read one too many romance novels before I was born." He rewarded her with a grin that showcased his perfectly white teeth.

"Uhg! Forget it." Jonathan dropped his empty beer bottle on the table. "This place is too busy. Alex always picks the busiest places."

"It's Friday night in Chicago. Every restaurant is too busy." Jessica pointed out.

Royce turned in his chair and raised his hand. A short blonde waitress wearing too much makeup arrived at their table. Jonathan watched in awe, barely able to sputter out his order. Jessica pretended not to notice the eagerness of the waitress, or how she fawned over Royce. The buttons on her blouse threatened to burst off and injure one of them if she pushed her chest out any further at him.

Alex returned to the table as the drinks arrived. "Jess, I was afraid you wouldn't make it tonight. You said you've been buried all week." He sipped at his beer. "Jess works at McCannis and Son's firm. Trying to take down some big corporation for screwing with the employee's 401(k)s."

Royce raised an eyebrow in her direction. His blue eyes darkened. "Not another Enron, I hope."

"No, nothing that serious. Just some corrupt bastards messing with balances and withholdings." Jessica waved a hand in the air. "I'm just a paralegal, not the attorney. Alex makes everything I do sound more important than it is." She felt the blush spread over her cheeks and cursed herself.

"Oh, please!" Alex rolled his eyes. "You carry that asshole you work for. If it weren't for you, he'd have lost his partnership and most of his cases last year."

Jessica laughed off his praise and squeezed his hand. "The big brother I never had." She changed the subject by looking over at Kelly and asking about her day.

Kelly worked at UIC; however, she was now the professor, instead of the student. Kelly loved to talk about her job. Royce made the perfect new audience, and Jessica relaxed back in her chair and watched the show.

Kelly grew more desperate by the day to find her soul mate. She wanted a family, the perfect husband, and exactly two children, one boy and one girl. It was her life's goal. By achieving that, her life would be complete.

Royce listened dutifully, occasionally glancing at Jessica to gauge her expressions. Jessica tried to ignore his stares, but she couldn't lie to herself that his glances weren't making her warm under the collar.

He was very attractive; she couldn't lie about that either. Too attractive. He would be interested in only one thing, and then he'd leave, or he'd not be interested in her from the start. She tried to focus on Kelly, but having heard the rant a dozen times before, Jessica found it very difficult to concentrate.

"What do you do?" Kelly finally turned the conversation over to Royce.

"Oh, he's the new VP of marketing."

"Alex, he's a big boy. Let him answer." Erin reached over the table and playfully slapped Alex's hand.

Jonathan watched her with an odd expression.

"Well, he's right. Just moved here from New York." Royce scanned the menu.

"You don't have an accent." Jessica pointed out with skepticism. She couldn't help herself. She shrugged off the glare from Alex.

"No, I'm originally from here. Well, the northern suburbs," he explained with a casual tone, his eyes locked with hers.

Jessica tore her gaze from him and looked at Alex. "I thought you were up for that promotion."

He shook his head. "No, I'm up for the advertising department."

"Isn't it the same thing?"

"Yes and no." Alex shrugged. "Let's talk about something not work related." He looked over at Jonathan for his assistance.

The talk turned casual. Jonathan and Alex made plans for tailgating during the football season. Kelly smiled like a star-struck teen at Royce, who continued to be polite, while stealing glances at Jessica.

"You are in sales or the craft of advertising?" She found herself asking over her latte. The meal was well past gone and the dessert plate Alex had ordered for the table remained in the center of the table scarcely touched.

"I prefer the craft. I went to school originally for writing. Advertising didn't seem too far off from writing fiction at the time. However, business being what it is, there isn't much in the way of craft anymore. Now it's all about projections, sales numbers, and profit margins." He sounded forlorn. She suspected he longed for something he'd left behind in the past. She knew that feeling intimately.

"So you started out as a writer and ended up VP of Marketing. Not too bad, I guess." She could hear the sarcasm in her own voice and chastised herself for not being better at hiding her annoyance for the opposite sex. Alex reminded her relentlessly that not all people of the male persuasion were bad, and she'd do better in life not to hate men in general.

"Royce, how is it that you have not been snatched up by some beautiful woman? I mean New York is crawling with them." Kelly blurted out and didn't even have the decency to look embarrassed over her statement.

"Kelly, not everyone is out looking for the one and only," Jessica interjected. "I'm sure there were plenty of women in New York who Royce enjoyed the company of, but that doesn't mean he had to settle down with any of them." She maintained her composure surprisingly well when Alex kicked her shin with the tip of his booted foot.

"Actually, there was one woman in New York. I only lived there for three years. She and I parted ways a few months back." Royce kept his eyes focused on Jessica as he answered, then swung a carefree smile toward Kelly.

"You'll have to forgive Jessica. She doesn't believe love exists anymore." Erin pushed her dessert plate away.

"Perhaps she hasn't met the right sort of man," Royce stated in a flat voice.

"That's probably right." Alex looked at his watch. "Well, kids, I gotta run." He shoved back from the table and whipped his overcoat on. "Do you want to share a cab?" he questioned Royce.

"No, thanks. I don't live too far from here, maybe five blocks or so. I think I'll hoof it while the weather holds out."

"Fair enough. Jess, I'll call you in the morning." Alex leaned down and placed a chaste kiss on her cheek before waving to the rest of the group and taking his leave.

"Did he just stiff us with the bill?" Kelly watched

Alex leave.

"No." Jessica laughed. "He'd never do that. He's going to stop at the front and pay the whole damn tab." She reached behind her and started to put her arms in the sleeves of her coat.

Alex earned more money than all of them combined. He found the fact embarrassing and hated to talk about it.

Jessica felt Royce watching her with fascination as she put her coat on while it remained draped over the chair. She stood from the table, and the coat conformed to her body perfectly.

"What?" She looked around to see if she had dropped or torn something.

"Nothing." He shook his head with a grin.

"I'm going to head out. I'll see you guys next Friday. Kelly, your pick, don't forget. And please, no where crazy. I'm still surprised we didn't all die from that hole in the wall you took us to last time."

"Hey, that Indian place was great." Kelly pouted.

"Okay. I'll see you later." Jessica waved at the group. She stepped to the side to allow Royce more room as he stood from his chair.

"It was very nice meeting everyone." Royce nodded to the group then turned to Jessica. "May I walk you to the door?" he asked in a gentleman's voice.

She looked him over and shrugged. No point getting her hopes up. "Sure. We're both headed that way anyway." She ignored the scowl on Kelly's face. She would call her later.

Jessica walked ahead of Royce and only noticed his presence when he reached in front of her to move a chair from blocking her way. She mumbled a thank you and continued on toward the door. Before she could open it, he reached in front of her again and pushed it open, letting in the sharp, cool air.

"Hail a cab?" He started to raise his hand, and she had no doubt that several cabs would pull over the instant he did so. He had an air of authority about him, as though anything he commanded would simply happen for him. She'd met very few men who held themselves with such confidence as he did.

"I walked. Just a few blocks," she stated as she buttoned her coat, holding her purse tightly between her arm and body.

"Which way?" He dropped his hand.

"That way." She pointed north and was rewarded with a grin that displayed a small dimple on his right cheek, which she hadn't seen during dinner.

"Me too. Okay if I join you?" He slid his hands into his pockets.

She swallowed. "Sure. Why not." She shrugged again. A walk was harmless.

They walked in silence for the first block. Neither seemed to know what to say or how to begin a conversation. Jessica felt his eyes on her, but continued to look straight ahead of her. It had been a while since she spent this much time alone with a man.

Royce broke the silence by inquiring about her work. He gave her his full attention, asking questions when he didn't understand something she said. He didn't just nod and daydream like most of the men she'd dated.

She began to relax by the time they made their way onto her block. She focused on him as he told her about his new position. He hadn't been looking for an executive job when he'd applied with Alex's company, and he seemed cautiously optimistic about the new position.

She paused outside the steps to her apartment building to listen to him finish and noticed a couple coming down the stairs of the next building. The woman, a beautiful brunette, walked with a little limp as though she felt tender with her movements. The man walked behind her as a cab pulled to the curb, and he opened the door for her.

Then he slid his hand under her hair and cupped the back of her head, pulling her to his lips. They exchanged a passionate kiss, which he broke off, causing her to look disappointed. He laid a hand on a pendant she wore around her neck and said something to her that Jessica couldn't make out. The woman's smile spoke of pure happiness—raw joy—as though he had just said the most romantic thing in the world to her.

Jessica heard the woman say, "Yes, Sir. Thank you," before she sunk into the cab. The man paid the driver and waved to her as she pulled away.

"Jessica…Jessica…" Royce's voice pulled her back to him.

"I'm…wow. I'm sorry. I was…" She watched the man skip up his steps and go back into his building.

"You were eavesdropping on that couple." Royce's eyes glistened with laughter, his lips curving up at the ends.

"Yes." She laughed. "It's just…they seemed so entwined with each other."

"Some couples are actually happy together." He pointed out, leaning against the railing of the stairs.

"She didn't call him by name. She called him Sir. Isn't that an odd thing to call your lover?" she asked, using her forefinger to push a lock of hair behind her ear.

Royce's expression changed. The laughter in his eyes dropped and was replaced with a mysterious look of seriousness, as though her words struck a nerve.

"No, it's not odd at all. To some, it's just as endearing as calling him honey or sweetheart—perhaps more intimate than those words." His voice was smooth, firm. She wasn't sure if she had offended him, or he was trying to teach her something.

She swung her eyes to the door of the man's apartment and back to Royce. There was more here than she knew about.

"I should probably get inside. I'm getting cold. Thank you for walking me home." She nodded and began to walk up her steps.

"You aren't one for hugs and such."

She stopped midstride and looked back at him. "That's a weird thing to say." She faced him from two steps up.

He looked up at her. "Not really. I noticed when we left the restaurant you didn't hug anyone goodbye, and Alex's kiss made you feel awkward."

She didn't know what to say to him. He was right. "Not every woman likes to be hugged and kissed all the time." She shot back at him, and he smiled. Not a pleasing smile, but one of knowledge, as though she had just told him some secret he was looking for.

"You're right." He pushed off the railing. "Do you think we could have dinner together? Tomorrow maybe?"

She looked down at him with narrow eyes. "I don't know."

"I'm not proposing marriage. I'm asking you to dinner." He pointed out with a grin. There was his dimple again.

"Okay. One less night of ramen noodles is fine with me." She shrugged, and he shook his head.

"You are not as complicated as you would like everyone to believe, Jessica. I'll pick you up at seven."

Before she could respond to his first comment, he turned and walked away. She watched him for a moment then ran up the steps to the safety of her apartment.

Royce walked into his two bedroom apartment unsure of what he might find when he turned the lights on. The woman he'd spoken of at dinner had been more of serious break-up than he'd let on. She hadn't taken the split well and was still trying to persuade him to take her back.

Melody hadn't been a flimsy dalliance, but she was not what he wanted for the rest of his life either. The time came when he had to break off their relationship because he could tell she was looking for more than he was able to give her. The job offer in Chicago could not have come at a more convenient time. Unfortunately, Melody had found out from a mutual friend where he had landed and began sending "housewarming" gifts once a week.

When he called to thank her for the first gift, a new set of wine glasses, he kept the conversation short. He deliberately called during her lunch break, knowing she'd have to run into a meeting shortly after the call began. He sent a thank you card after the second gift—a set of martini glasses—and assured her no more gifts were required. The third gift, a set of shot glasses, received no reply from him at all.

He breathed a sigh of relief when he turned on the lights and didn't see a package anywhere in sight. He tossed his keys on the nearest table and went to his bedroom in search of something more comfortable to wear.

He didn't quite know exactly what to make of Jessica other than he found himself drawn to her. Her attempt to keep her attitude aloof and offer him indifference had failed. He'd noticed the tapping of her fingers on the table when she'd felt his stare on her. She'd wanted to look at him, wanted to see what he was up to, but she'd forced herself to keep her eyes elsewhere.

The peck Alex gave her before he left had made her uncomfortable. She'd wiped the kiss from her cheek as soon as he'd turned away, and she'd looked awkward, as though her brother had just made a pass at her. She wasn't one for open affection, no hugs to all of her friends as she left, just a simple wave of her hand. But she had reacted warmly to the couple outside her apartment building. She had watched intently as they'd had their passionate embrace, and she'd listened with keen precision as the woman spoke to her lover.

What an odd thing to call your lover, she had said.

He thought about how beautiful her voice would sound when she called him Sir for the first time.

Hidden Heart
Coming in 2014